Dora
Bruder

Dora Bruder with her mother and father

Dora
Bruder

PATRICK MODIANO

Translated from the French
by Joanna Kilmartin

UNIVERSITY OF CALIFORNIA PRESS

BERKELEY | LOS ANGELES | LONDON

University of California Press
Oakland, California

© 1999 by The Regents of the University of California
Translation © 1999 by Joanna Kilmartin

Originally published as *Dora Bruder* in 1997 by Éditions
Gallimard, Paris. Copyright © Editions Gallimard Paris, 1997

First Paperback printing, 2015

Library of Congress Cataloging-in-Publication Data

Modiano, Patrick, 1945–
  [Dora Bruder. English]
  Dora Bruder/Patrick Modiano ; translated from the French
by Joanna Kilmartin.
    p. cm.
  ISBN 978-0-520-21878-9
  1. Modiano, Patrick, 1945– . 2. Bruder, Dora, 1926–1942?
3. Holocaust, Jewish (1939–1945). I. Kilmartin, Joanna.
II. Title.
PQ2673.O3Z46413 1999
940.53'18'092—dc21   98-33890
[b]   CIP

Printed in the United States of America

9 8 7 6 5 4 3
19 18 17 16 15

The publisher gratefully acknowledges the contribution to this book provided by the Literature in Translation Endowment of the Associates of the University of California Press, which is supported by a generous gift from Joan Palevsky.

XIIe Arrondissement (detail)

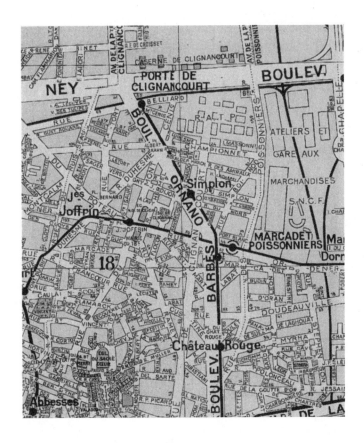

XVIIIᵉ Arrondissement (detail)

Dora
Bruder

. . . .

E IGHT YEARS AGO, IN AN OLD COPY OF *PARIS-SOIR* DATED
31 December 1941, a heading on page 3 caught my eye:
"From Day to Day."[1] Below this, I read:

PARIS

Missing, a young girl, Dora Bruder, age 15, height 1 m
55, oval-shaped face, gray-brown eyes, gray sports jacket,
maroon pullover, navy blue skirt and hat, brown gym
shoes. Address all information to M. and Mme Bruder,
41 Boulevard Ornano, Paris.

I had long been familiar with that area of the Boulevard
Ornano. As a child, I would accompany my mother to the
Saint-Ouen flea markets. We would get off the bus either at
the Porte de Clignancourt or, occasionally, outside the 18th
arrondissement town hall. It was always a Saturday or Sunday
afternoon.

In winter, on the tree-shaded sidewalk outside Clignancourt barracks, the fat photographer with round spectacles
and a lumpy nose would set up his tripod camera among the
stream of passers-by, offering "souvenir photos." In summer,
he stationed himself on the boardwalk at Deauville, outside
the Bar du Soleil. There, he found plenty of customers. But at
the Porte de Clignancourt, the passers-by showed little incli-

---

1. "D'hier à aujord'hui."

nation to be photographed. His overcoat was shabby and he had a hole in one shoe.

I remember the Boulevard Ornano and the Boulevard Barbès, deserted, one sunny afternoon in May 1958. There were groups of riot police at each crossroads, because of the situation in Algeria.

I was in this neighborhood in the winter of 1965. I had a girlfriend who lived in the Rue Championnet. Ornano 49–20.

Already, by that time, the Sunday stream of passers-by outside the barracks must have swept away the fat photographer, but I never went back to check. What had they been used for, those barracks?[2] I had been told that they housed colonial troops.

January 1965. Dusk came around six o'clock to the crossroads of the Boulevard Ornano and the Rue Championnet. I merged into that twilight, into those streets, I was nonexistent.

The last café at the top of the Boulevard Ornano, on the right, was called the Verse Toujours.[3] There was another, on the left, at the corner of the Boulevard Ney, with a jukebox. The Ornano-Championnet crossroads had a pharmacy and two cafés, the older of which was on the corner of the Rue Duhesme.

The time I've spent, waiting in those cafés . . . First thing

---

2. During the Occupation of Paris, Clignancourt barracks housed French volunteers in the Waffen SS. See David Pryce-Jones, *Parus ub the Third Reich*, Collins, 1981.

3. "Keep pouring, nonstop."

in the morning, when it was still dark. Early in the evening, as night fell. Later on, at closing time . . .

On Sunday evening, an old black sports car—a Jaguar, I think—was parked outside the nursery school on the Rue Championnet. It had a plaque at the rear: Disabled Ex-Serviceman. The presence of such a car in this neighborhood surprised me. I tried to imagine what its owner might look like.

After nine o'clock at night, the boulevard is deserted. I can still see lights at the mouth of Simplon métro station and, almost opposite, in the foyer of the Cinéma Ornano 43. I've never really noticed the building beside the cinema, number 41, even though I've been passing it for months, for years. From 1965 to 1968. Address all information to M. and Mme Bruder, 41 Boulevard Ornano, Paris.

FROM DAY TO DAY. WITH THE PASSAGE OF TIME, I FIND, perspectives become blurred, one winter merging into another. That of 1965 and that of 1942.

In 1965, I knew nothing of Dora Bruder. But now, thirty years on, it seems to me that those long waits in the cafés at the Ornano crossroads, those unvarying itineraries—the Rue du Mont-Cenis took me back to some hotel on the Butte Montmartre: the Roma or the Alsina or the Terrass, Rue Caulaincourt—and the fleeting impressions I have retained: snatches of conversation heard on a spring evening, beneath the trees in the Square Clignancourt, and again, in winter, on the way down to Simplon and the Boulevard Ornano, all that was not simply due to chance. Perhaps, though not yet fully aware of it, I was following the traces of Dora Bruder and her parents. Already, below the surface, they were there.

I'm trying to search for clues, going far, far back in time. When I was about twelve, on those visits to the Clignancourt flea markets with my mother, on the right, at the top of one of those aisles bordered by stalls, the Marché Malik, or the Vernaison, there was a young Polish Jew who sold suitcases . . . Luxury suitcases, in leather or crocodile skin, cardboard suitcases, traveling bags, cabin trunks labeled with the names of transatlantic companies—all heaped one on top of the other. His was an open-air stall. He was never without a cigarette dangling from the corner of his lips and, one afternoon, he had offered me one.

Occasionally, I would go to one of the cinemas on the Boulevard Ornano. To the Clignancourt Palace at the top of the boulevard, next to the Verse Toujours. Or to the Ornano 43.

Later, I discovered that the Ornano 43 was a very old cinema. It had been rebuilt in the thirties, giving it the air of an ocean liner. I returned to the area in May 1996. A shop had replaced the cinema. You cross the Rue Hermel and find yourself outside 41 Boulevard Ornano, the address given in the notice about the search for Dora Bruder.

A five-story building, late nineteenth century. Together with number 39, it forms a single block, enclosed by the boulevard, the top of the Rue Hermel, and the Rue Simplon, which runs along the back of both buildings. These are matching. A plaque on number 39 gives the name of the architect, a man named Pierrefeu, and the date of construction: 1881. The same must be true of number 41.

Before the war, and up to the beginning of the fifties, number 41 had been a hotel, as had number 39, calling itself the Hôtel Lion d'Or. Number 39 also had a café-restaurant before the war, owned by a man named Gazal. I haven't found out the name of the hotel at number 41. Listed under this address, in the early fifties, is the Société Ornano and Studios Ornano: Montmartre 12–54. Also, both then and before the war, a café with a proprietor by the name of Marchal. This café no longer exists. Would it have been to the right or the left of the porte cochère?

This opens onto a longish corridor. At the far end, a staircase leads off to the right.

. . . .

IT TAKES TIME FOR WHAT HAS BEEN ERASED TO RESURFACE. Traces survive in registers, and nobody knows where these registers are hidden, and who has custody of them, and whether or not these custodians are willing to let you see them. Or perhaps they have quite simply forgotten that these registers exist.

All it takes is a little patience.

Thus, I came to learn that Dora Bruder and her parents were already living in the hotel on the Boulevard Ornano in 1937 and 1938. They had a room with kitchenette on the fifth floor, the level at which an iron balcony encircles both buildings. The fifth floor has some ten windows. Of these, two or three give onto the boulevard, and the rest onto the Rue Hermel or, at the back, the Rue Simplon.

When I revisited the neighborhood on that day in May 1996, rusting shutters were closed over the two end fifth-floor windows overlooking the Rue Simplon, and outside, on the balcony, I noticed a collection of miscellaneous objects, seemingly long abandoned there.

During the last three or four years before the war, Dora Bruder would have been enrolled at one of the local state secondary schools. I wrote to ask if her name was to be found on the school registers, addressing my letter to the head of each:

8 Rue Ferdinand-Flocon
20 Rue Hermel

7 Rue Championnet

61 Rue de Clignancourt

All replied politely. None had found this name on the list of their prewar pupils. In the end, the head of the former girls' school at 69 Rue Championnet suggested that I come and consult the register for myself. One of these days, I shall. But I'm of two minds. I want to go on hoping that her name is there. It was the school nearest to where she lived.

It took me four years to discover her exact date of birth: 25 February 1926. And a further two years to find out her place of birth: Paris, 12th arrondissement. But I am a patient man. I can wait for hours in the rain.

One Friday afternoon in February 1996 I went to the 12th arrondissement Register Office. The registrar—a young man—handed me a form:

To be completed by the person applying for the certificate. Fill in your

Surname

First name

Address

I require a full copy of the Birth Certificate for

Surname   BRUDER   First Name   DORA

Date of birth: 25 February 1926

Check if you are:

☐ The person in question   ☐ Son or daughter

☐ Father or mother   ☐ Husband or wife

☐ Grandfather or grandmother

☐ Legal representative (You have power of attorney, and an identity card for the person in question)

No persons other than the above may be supplied with a copy of a Birth Certificate.

I signed the form and handed it back to him. After reading it through, he said that he was unable to supply me with a standard birth certificate: I bore no legal relationship whatever to the person in question.

At first, I took him for one of those sentinels of oblivion whose role is to guard a shameful secret and deny access to anybody seeking to uncover the least trace of a person's existence. But he was a decent fellow. He advised me to go to the Palais de Justice, 2 Boulevard du Palais, and apply for a special exemption from the Superintendent Registrar, Section 3, 5th floor, Staircase 5, Room 501. Monday to Friday, 2 to 4 P.M.

I was about to enter the main courtyard through the big iron gates at 2 Boulevard du Palais when a functionary directed me to another entrance a little farther down: the same as that for the Sainte-Chapelle. Tourists were waiting in a line between the barriers and I wanted to go straight on, through the porch, but another functionary gestured at me impatiently to line up with the rest.

At the back of the foyer, regulations required you to empty your pockets of anything metal. I had nothing on me except a bunch of keys. This I was supposed to place on a sort of conveyor belt for collection on the far side of a glass partition, but for a moment I couldn't think what to do. My hesitation earned me a rebuke from another functionary. Was he a guard? A policeman? Was I also supposed to hand over my shoelaces, belt, wallet, as at the gates of a prison?

I crossed a courtyard, followed a corridor, and emerged into a vast concourse milling with men and women carrying black briefcases, some dressed in legal robes. I didn't dare ask them how to get to Staircase 5.

A guard seated at a table directed me to the back of the concourse. And here I entered a deserted hall whose high windows let in a dim, gray light. I searched every corner of this room without finding Staircase 5. I was seized with panic, with that sense of vertigo you have in bad dreams when you can't get to the station, time is running out and you are going to miss your train.

Twenty years before, I had had a similar experience. I had learned that my father was in hospital, in the Pitié-Salpêtrière. I hadn't seen him since the end of my adolescent years. I therefore decided to pay him an impromptu visit.

I remember wandering for hours through the vastness of that hospital in search of him. I found my way into ancient buildings, into communal wards lined with beds, I questioned nurses who gave me contradictory directions. I came to doubt my father's existence, passing and repassing that majestic church, and those spectral buildings, unchanged since the seventeenth century, which, for me, evoke Manon Lescaut and the era when, under the sinister name General Hospital, the place was used as a prison for prostitutes awaiting deportation to Louisiana. I tramped the paved courtyards till dusk. It was impossible to find my father. I never saw him again.

But I found Staircase 5 in the end. I climbed several flights. A row of offices. I was directed to Room 501. A bored-looking woman with short hair asked me what I wanted.

Curtly, she informed me that to obtain particulars of a birth certificate I should write to the Public Prosecutor,[1] Department B, 14 Quai des Orfèvres, Paris 3.

Three weeks later, I had a reply.

At nine ten P.M. on twenty-five February nineteen hundred twenty-six, at 15 Rue Santerre, a female child, Dora, was born to Ernest Bruder, unskilled laborer, born Vienna (Austria) twenty-one May eighteen hundred ninety-nine, and to his wife, Cécile Burdej, housewife, born Budapest (Hungary) seventeen April nineteen hundred seven, both domiciled at 2 Avenue Liégeard, Sevran (Seine-et-Oise). Registered at three thirty P.M. on twenty-seven February nineteen hundred twenty-six on the declaration of Gaspard Meyer, aged seventy-three, employed and domiciled at 76 Rue de Picpus, having been present at the birth, who has read and signed it with Us, Auguste Guillaume Rossi, Deputy Mayor, 12th arrondissement, Paris.

---

1. An official who has a number of nonjudicial functions in France.

15 Rue Santerre is the address of the Rothschild Hospital. Many children of poor Jewish families, recent immigrants to France, were born in its maternity ward around the same time as Dora. Seemingly, on that Thursday of 25 February 1926, Ernest Bruder had been unable to get time off from work in order to register his daughter himself at the 12th arrondissement town hall. Perhaps there is a register somewhere with more information about the Gaspard Meyer who had signed the birth certificate. 76 Rue de Picpus, where he was "employed and domiciled," is the address of the Rothschild Hospice, an establishment for the old and indigent.

In that winter of 1926 all trace of Dora Bruder and her parents peters out in Sevran, the suburb to the northeast, bordering the Ourcq canal. One day I shall go to Sevran, but I fear that, as in all suburbs, houses and streets will have changed beyond recognition. Here are the names of a few businesses and inhabitants of the Avenue Liégeard dating from that period: the Trianon de Freinville occupied number 24. Was this a café? A cinema? The Île-de-France wine cellars at number 31. There was a Dr. Jorand at number 9, a pharmacist, Platel, at number 30.

The Avenue Liégeard where Dora's parents lived was part of a built-up area that sprawled across the communities of Sevran, Livry-Gargan, and Aulnay-sous-Bois and was known as Freinville.[2] It had grown up around the Westinghouse Brake Factory, established there at the beginning of the cen-

---

2. The equivalent of Brakesville, from *frein,* a brake.

14

tury. A working-class area. In the thirties, it had tried to gain its autonomy, without success, and so had remained a dependency of the three adjoining communities. But it had its own railway station nevertheless: Freinville.

In that winter of 1926, Ernest Bruder, Dora's father, is sure to have been employed at the Westinghouse Brake Factory.

ERNEST BRUDER, BORN VIENNA, AUSTRIA, 21 MAY 1899. His childhood would have been spent in that city's Jewish quarter, Leopoldstadt. His own parents were almost certainly natives of Galicia or Bohemia or Moravia, having come, like the majority of Vienna's Jews, from the eastern provinces of the Empire.

I had turned twenty in Vienna, in 1965, also the year when I was frequenting the Clignancourt districts. I lived on the Taubenstummengasse, behind the Karlskirche. My first few nights were spent in a seedy hotel near the Western Station. I have memories of summer evenings spent in Sievering and Grinzing, and of parks where bands were playing. And, not far from Heilingenstadt, of a shack in the middle of some sort of allotment. Everything was closed on those July weekends, even the Café Hawelka. The city was deserted. Tramlines glistened in the sunlight, crisscrossing the northwestern districts as far as Pötzleinsdorf Park.

Some day, I shall go back to Vienna, a city I haven't seen for over thirty years. Perhaps I shall find Ernest Bruder's birth certificate in the Register Office of Vienna's Jewish community. I shall learn his father's first name, occupation, and birthplace, his mother's first name and maiden name. And whereabouts they had lived in that zone of the 2d district, somewhere between the Northern Station, the Prater, and the Danube.

Child and adolescent, he would have known the Prater, with its cafés, and its theater, the home of the Budapester. And the Sweden Bridge. And the courtyard of the Commodities Exchange, near the Taborstrasse. And the market square of the Carmelites.

In 1919, his life as a twenty-year-old in Vienna had been harder than mine. Following the first defeats of the Austrian army, tens of thousands of refugees fleeing from Galicia, Bukovina, and the Ukraine had arrived in successive waves to crowd into the slums around the Northern Station. A city adrift, cut off from an empire that had ceased to exist. Ernest Bruder must have been indistinguishable from those bands of unemployed roaming the streets of shuttered shops.

Or did he come from a less poverty-stricken background than the refugees from the east? The son of a Taborstrasse shopkeeper, perhaps? How are we to know?

On a file card, one of thousands in an index created some twenty years later to facilitate the roundup of Jews during the Occupation, and which still lies around to this day at the Veterans' Administration, Ernest Bruder is described as "French legionnaire, 2d class." So he must have enlisted in the Foreign Legion, though I have no means of knowing precisely when. 1919? 1920?

A man enlisted for five years. He didn't even need to go to France, it was enough to visit a French consulate. Was that what Ernest Bruder did, in Austria? Or was he already in France by then? Either way, along with other Germans and

Austrians in his situation, he was probably sent to the barracks at Belfort and Nancy, where they were not exactly received with open arms. Then it was Marseille and the Fort Saint-Jean, where the reception was cooler still. After that, the troopship: in Morocco, it seemed, Lyautey was short of thirty thousand troops.

I'm trying to reconstitute Ernest Bruder's tour of duty. The bounty, handed out at Sidi Bel Abbès. The condition of most enlisted men—Germans, Austrians, Russians, Rumanians, Bulgarians—is so miserable that they are dazed by the idea of receiving a bounty. They can't believe their luck. Hastily, they stuff the money into their pockets, as if it might be taken back from them. Then comes the training, long runs over the dunes, interminable marches under a leaden African sun. For volunteers from Central Europe, like Ernest Bruder, it is hard going: they have been undernourished throughout adolescence, owing to four years of wartime rationing.

Next, the barracks at Meknès, Fez, or Marrakesh. They are sent on operations intended to pacify the still rebellious territories of Morocco.

April 1920. Fighting at Bekrit and the Ras-Tarcha. June 1921. Legion battalion under Major Lambert engaged in the Djebel Hayane. March 1922. Fighting at Chouf-ech-Cherg. Captain Roth. May 1922. Fighting at Tizi Adni. Nicolas battalion. April 1923. Fighting at Arbala, and in the Taza corridor. May 1923. Heavy fighting for the Talrant Bab-Brida, taken under intense fire by Naegelin's legionnaires. On the night of the 26th, in a surprise attack, the Naegelin battal-

ion occupies the Ichendirt massif. June 1923. Fighting at Ta-
dout. Naegelin battalion takes the ridge. Legionnaires raise
the tricolor over an important casbah to the sound of bu-
gles. Fighting at Oued Athia, where the Barrière battalion has
to make two bayonet charges. Buchsenschutz battalion takes
entrenched positions on the pinnacle south of Bou-Khamouj.
Fighting in the El-Mers basin. July 1923. Fighting on the Im-
mouzer plateau. Cattin battalion. Buchsenschutz battalion.
Susini and Jenoudet battalions. August 1923. Fighting at
Oued Tamghilt.

At night, in this landscape of stone-strewn sand, did he
dream of Vienna, the city of his birth, and the chestnut trees
of the Hauptallee? The file of Ernest Bruder, "French legionnaire, 2d class" also indicates: "100% disabled." In which of
these battles was he wounded?

At the age of twenty-five, he was back on the streets of Paris.
The Legion must have released him from his engagement because of his war wound. I don't suppose he talked about it to
anybody. Not that anybody would have been interested. I'm
almost sure he didn't receive a disability pension. He was never
given French nationality. In fact, I've seen his disability mentioned only once, and that was in one of the police files de-
signed to facilitate the roundups during the Occupation.

IN 1924, ERNEST BRUDER MARRIED A YOUNG WOMAN OF seventeen, Cécile Burdej, born 17 April 1907 in Budapest. I don't know where this marriage took place, nor do I know the names of their witnesses. How did they happen to meet? Cécile Burdej had arrived in Paris the year before, with her parents, her brother, and her four sisters. A Jewish family of Russian origin, they had probably settled in Budapest at the beginning of the century.

Life in Budapest and Vienna being equally hard after the First World War, they had had to flee west yet again. They ended up in Paris, at the Jewish refuge in the Rue Lamarck. Within a month of their arrival, three of the girls, aged fourteen, twelve, and ten, were dead of typhoid fever.

Were Cécile and Ernest Bruder already living in the Avenue Liégeard, Sevran, at the time of their marriage? Or in a hotel in Paris? For the first years of their marriage, after Dora's birth, they always lived in hotel rooms.

They are the sort of people who leave few traces. Virtually anonymous. Inseparable from those Paris streets, those suburban landscapes where, by chance, I discovered that they had lived. Often, what I know about them amounts to no more than a simple address. And such topographical precision contrasts with what we shall never know about their life—this blank, this mute block of the unknown.

I tracked down Ernest and Cécile Bruder's niece. I talked to her on the telephone. The memories that she retains of them are those of childhood, at once fuzzy and sharp. She remembers her uncle's gentleness, his kindness. It was she who gave me the few details that I have noted down about their family. She had heard it said that before they lived in the hotel on the Boulevard Ornano, Ernest, Cécile, and their daughter, Dora, had lived in another hotel. In a street off the Rue des Poissonniers. Looking at the street map, I read her out a succession of names. Yes, that was it, the Rue Polonceau. But she had never heard any mention of Sevran, nor Freinville, nor the Westinghouse factory.

It is said that premises retain some stamp, however faint, of their previous inhabitants. Stamp: an imprint, hollow or in relief. Hollow, I should say, in the case of Ernest and Cécile Bruder, of Dora. I have a sense of absence, of emptiness, whenever I find myself in a place where they have lived.

Two hotels, for that date, in the Rue Polonceau: the tenant of one, at number 49, was called Roquette. In the telephone directory he appears under Hôtel Vin. The other, at number 32, was owned by a Charles Campazzi. As hotels, they had a bad reputation. Today, they no longer exist.

Often, around 1968, I would follow the boulevards as far as the arches of the overhead métro. My starting point was the Place Blanche. In December, a traveling fair occupied the open ground. Its lights grew dimmer the nearer you got to the Boulevard de la Chapelle. At the time, I knew nothing of Dora

Bruder and her parents. I remember that I had a peculiar sensation as I hugged the wall of Lariboisière Hospital, and again on crossing the railway tracks, as though I had penetrated the darkest part of Paris. But it was merely the contrast, after the dazzling lights of the Boulevard de Clichy, with the black, interminable wall, the penumbra beneath the métro arches . . .

Nowadays, on account of the railway lines, the proximity of the Gare du Nord and the rattle of the high-speed trains overhead, I still think of this part of the Boulevard de la Chapelle as a network of escape routes . . . A place where nobody would stay for long. A crossroads, where everybody went their separate ways to the four points of the compass.

All the same, I made a note of local schools where, if they still exist, I might find Dora Bruder's name in the register:

Nursery school: 3 Rue Saint-Luc
Primary schools for girls: 11 Rue Cavé, 43 Rue des
  Poissonniers, Impasse d'Oran

ND, AT THE PORTE DE CLIGNANCOURT, THE YEARS
slipped by till the outbreak of war. I know nothing about
the Bruders during this time. Was Cécile already working as
a "furrier's seamstress," or rather, as it says in the files, "sal-
aried garment worker"? Her niece thinks that she was employed in a workshop near the Rue de Ruisseau, but she can't
be sure. Was Ernest Bruder still working as an unskilled laborer, if not at the Westinghouse factory in Freinville, then
elsewhere, in some other suburb? Or had he too found work
in a garment workshop in Paris? Next to the words trade or
profession on the file that they had drawn up on him during
the Occupation, and on which I had read "French legionnaire,
2d class, 100% disabled," it says "None."

A few photographs from this period. The earliest, their
wedding day. They are seated, their elbows resting on a sort
of pedestal. She is enveloped in a long white veil that trails
to the floor and seems to be knotted at her left ear. He wears
tails with a white bow tie. A photograph with their daughter, Dora. They are seated, Dora standing between them: she
can't be more than two years old. A photograph of Dora,
surely taken after a special school assembly. She is aged twelve
or thereabouts and wears a white dress and ankle socks. She
holds a book in her right hand. Her hair is crowned by a cir-
clet of what appear to be white flowers. Her left hand rests
on the edge of an enormous white cube patterned with rows

of black geometric motifs, clearly a studio prop. Another photograph, taken in the same place at the same period, perhaps on the same day: the floor tiles are recognizable, as is the big white cube with black geometric motifs on which Cécile Bruder is perched. Dora stands on her left, in a high-necked dress, her left arm bent across her body so as to place her hand on her mother's shoulder. In another photograph with her mother, Dora is about twelve years old, her hair shorter than in the previous picture. They are standing in front of what appears to be an old wall, though it must be one of the photographer's screens. Both wear black dresses with a white collar. Dora stands slightly in front and to the right of her mother. An oval-shaped photograph in which Dora is slightly older—thirteen or fourteen, longer hair— and all three are in single file, their faces turned toward the camera: first Dora and her mother, both in white blouses, then Ernest Bruder, in jacket and tie. A photograph of Cécile Bruder in front of what appears to be a suburban house. The lefthand wall in the foreground is covered in a mass of ivy. She is sitting on the edge of three concrete steps. She wears a light summer dress. In the background, the silhouette of a child with her back to the camera, her arms and legs bare, wearing either a black cardigan or a bathing suit. Dora? And behind a wooden fence, the facade of another house, with a porch and a single upstairs window. Where could this be?

An earlier photograph of Dora alone, aged nine or ten. Caught in a ray of sunshine, entirely surrounded by shadow,

Dora Bruder with her mother

Dora Bruder with her mother and grandmother

she might be on a rooftop. Dressed in a white blouse and ankle socks, she stands, hand on hip, her right foot placed on
the concrete rim of what appears to be a large cage or aviary,
although, owing to the shadow, you can't make out the ani-
mals or birds confined there. These shadows and patches of
sunlight are those of a summer's day.

OTHER SUMMER DAYS WERE SPENT IN CLIGNANCOURT. Her parents would take Dora to the Cinéma Ornano 43. It was just across the street. Or did she go on her own? From a very young age, according to her cousin, she had been rebellious, independent, with an eye for the boys. The hotel room was far too cramped for three people.

As a child, she would have played in the Square Clignancourt. At times, this part of town seemed like a village. In the evenings, the neighbors would place their chairs outside and sit on the sidewalk for a chat. Or take a lemonade together on the café terrace. Sometimes men who could have been either real goatherds or else peddlers from the fairs would come by with a few goats and sell you tall glasses of milk for almost nothing. The froth gave you a white mustache.

At the Porte de Clignancourt, the toll house and gate.[1] To its left, between the flea market and the tall apartment blocks of the Boulevard Ney, an entire district of shacks, warehouses, acacias, and low-built houses, since pulled down. This wasteland had impressed me, aged fourteen. I thought I recognized it in two or three photographs, taken in winter: a kind of esplanade, a passing bus in sight. A truck at a standstill,

---

1. One of the 18th-c. gates (*barrières*) in the fortifications of Paris; originally control points for game, later also used for goods subject to excise tax, they were abolished in the late 1920s.

seemingly forever. Waiting beside an expanse of snow, a trailer and a black horse. And in the far background, the dim masses of high buildings.

I remember experiencing for the first time that sense of emptiness that comes with the knowledge of what has been destroyed, razed to the ground. As yet, I was ignorant of the existence of Dora Bruder. Perhaps—in fact, I'm sure of it— she explored this zone that, for me, evokes secret lovers' trysts, pitiful moments of lost happiness. Here, reminders of the countryside still surfaced in the street names: Allée du Puits, Allée du Métro, Allée des Peupliers, Impasse des Chiens.

. . . .

ON 9 MAY 1940, AT THE AGE OF FOURTEEN, DORA BRUDER was enrolled in the boarding school of the Saint-Coeur-de-Marie, run by the Sisters of the Christian Schools of Divine Mercy[1] at 60–62 Rue de Picpus in the 12th arrondissement. The school register contains the following entry:

Name, last and first: Bruder, Dora
Date and place of birth: 26 February 1926, Paris 12
Parents: Ernest and Cécile Bruder *née* Brudej
Family status: legitimate
Date and conditions of admission: 9 May 1940. Full boarder
Date and reason for departure: 14 December 1941. Pupil
    has run away

What were her parents' reasons for sending her to this religious school? No doubt it was difficult living three to a room in the Boulevard Ornano hotel. I wonder if Ernest and Cécile Bruder, as ex-Austrians and "nationals of the Reich," were not threatened with a form of internment, Austria having ceased to exist in 1938 and become part of the "Reich."

In the autumn of 1939, men who were ex-Austrian or otherwise nationals of the "Reich" were interned in "assembly camps." They were divided into two categories: suspect and

---

1. The Écoles chrétiennes de la Miséricorde ran the boarding school (the Holy Heart of Mary).

non-suspect. Non-suspects were taken to Yves-du-Manoir stadium, in Colombes. Then, in December, they were included
with the group known as "foreign statute laborers." Was
Ernest Bruder among those laborers?

On 13 May 1940, four days after Dora Bruder's arrival
at the Saint-Coeur-de-Marie boarding school, ex-Austrian
women and nationals of the Reich were called up in their turn
and taken to the Vélodrome d'Hiver, where they were interned
for thirteen days. Then, with the approach of the German
army, they were transferred to the camp at Gurs, in the Basses-
Pyrénées. Was Cécile Bruder among those called up?

You were placed in bizarre categories you had never heard
of and with no relation to who you really were. You were called
up. You were interned. If only you could understand why.

I also wonder how Cécile and Ernest Bruder came to hear of
the Saint-Coeur-de-Marie boarding school. Who had advised
them to send Dora there?

I imagine that, by the age of fourteen, she must have given
proof of independence, and that the rebellious spirit her
cousin mentioned to me had already manifested itself. Her
parents felt that she was in need of discipline. For this, these
Jews chose a Christian institution. But were they themselves
practicing Jews? And what choice did they have? According
to the biographical note on the institution's Mother Superior
when Dora was a boarder there, the pupils at the Saint-Coeur-
de-Marie came from poor backgrounds: "Often they are or-
phans, or children dependent on social welfare, those to whom

Our Lord has always shown His special love." And, in a brochure about the Sisters of the Christian Schools of Divine Mercy, "The Saint-Coeur-de-Marie was called upon to render signal service to young children and adolescents from the capital's least fortunate families."

The teaching certainly went beyond the arts of housekeeping and sewing. The Sisters of the Christian Schools of Divine Mercy, whose mother house was the ancient abbey of Saint-Sauveur-le-Vicomte in Normandy, had founded the charitable institution of the Saint-Coeur-de-Marie, Rue de Picpus, in 1852. In those days, it was a vocational boarding school for five hundred girls, the daughters of working men's families, with a staff of seventy-five nuns.

At the time of the fall of France in June 1940, nuns and pupils were evacuated to the department of Maine-et-Loire. Dora would have left with them, on one of the last packed trains still running from the Gare d'Orsay and the Gare d'Austerlitz. They formed part of the endless procession of refugees on routes leading southward to the Loire.

July, and the return to Paris. Boarding-school life. I don't know what the school uniform consisted of. Was it, quite simply, the clothes listed in the notice about the search for Dora: maroon pullover, navy blue skirt, brown gym shoes? And, over this, a smock? I can more or less guess the daily timetable. Rise about six. Chapel. Classroom. Refectory. Classroom. Playground. Refectory. Classroom. Chapel. Dormitory. Day of rest, Sunday. I imagine that life behind those walls was hard for these girls for whom Our Lord had always shown His special love.

I have heard that the Sisters of the Christian Schools of Divine Mercy of the Rue de Picpus had established a holiday camp at Béthisy. Was it at Béthisy-Saint-Martin? Or Béthisy-Saint-Pierre? Both villages are near Senlis, in the Valois. Perhaps Dora Bruder and her classmates spent a few days there, in the summer of 1941.

The buildings of the Saint-Coeur-de-Marie no longer exist. Modern apartment blocks have taken their place, giving an idea of the vastness of the grounds. I don't possess a single photograph of the vanished school. On an old map of Paris, its site is marked "House of religious education." Four little squares and a cross symbolize the school buildings and chapel. And a long, narrow rectangle, extending from the Rue de Picpus to the Rue de la Gare-de-Reuilly, outlines the perimeter.

Opposite the school, on the other side of the Rue de Picpus, the map shows, successively, the houses of the Mère de Dieu congregation, then the Dames de l'Adoration, the Oratory of Picpus and the Picpus cemetery where, in the last months of the Terror, over one thousand victims of the guillotine were buried in a common grave. And on the same side of the street as the boarding school, almost an extension of it, the large property belonging to the Dames de Sainte-Clothilde. Then that of the Dames Diaconesses, where, one day, aged eighteen, I went for treatment. I remember the garden of the Diaconesses. I didn't know then that this establishment had served as a rehabilitation center for delinquent girls. Not unlike the Saint-Coeur-de-Marie. Not unlike the Bon-Pasteur. These institutions, where you were shut up, not knowing when or if you would be released, certainly rejoiced in some curious names: the Bon-Pasteur d'Angers. The Refuge de Darnetal. The sanctuary of Sainte-Madeleine de Limoges. The Solitude-de-Nazareth.

Solitude.

The Saint-Coeur-de-Marie, 60–62 Rue de Picpus, stood at the corner of the Rue de Picpus and the Rue de la Gare-de-Reuilly. In Dora's time, this street still had a countrified air. A high wall ran the length of its lefthand side, shaded by the school's trees.

The few details that I have managed to glean about these places, such as Dora Bruder would have seen them, day in, day out, for a year and a half, are as follows: the large garden ran the length of the Rue de la Gare-de-Reuilly, and the school buildings must have stood between it and the courtyard. Within this courtyard, hollowed out beneath rocks in the form of an imitation grotto, lay the burial vault of the Madre family, the school's benefactors.

I don't know if Dora Bruder made friends at the Saint-Coeur-de-Marie. Or if she kept to herself. Until such time as I have the testimony of one of her former classmates, I am reduced to conjecture. Today, in Paris, or somewhere in the suburbs, there must be a seventy-year-old woman who remembers her erstwhile neighbor in classroom or dormitory—a girl named Dora, age 15, height 1 m 55, oval-shaped face, gray-brown eyes, gray sports jacket, maroon pullover, navy blue skirt and hat, brown gym shoes.

In writing this book, I send out signals, like a lighthouse beacon in whose power to illuminate the darkness, alas, I have no faith. But I live in hope.

In those days, the Mother Superior of the Saint-Coeur-de-Marie was Mother Marie-Jean-Baptiste. She was born—so her biographical note tells us—in 1903. After her novitiate, she was sent to Paris, to the house of the Saint-Coeur-de-Marie, where she stayed for seventeen years, from 1929 to 1946. She was barely forty years old when Dora Bruder was a boarder there.

She was "independent and warm-hearted"—according to the biographical note—and "endowed with a strong personality." She died in 1985, three years before I knew of Dora Bruder's existence. She would certainly have remembered Dora—if only because the girl had run away. But, after all, what could she have told me? A few humdrum facts of daily existence? Warm-hearted or not, she certainly failed to divine what was going through Dora Bruder's head, neither how the girl was coping with boarding-school life nor how she reacted to chapel morning and evening, the fake grotto in the court-yard, the garden wall, the dormitory with its rows of beds.

I traced a woman who had entered the boarding school in 1942, a few months after Dora Bruder ran away. She was about ten years old at the time, younger than Dora. And her memories of the Saint-Coeur-de-Marie are merely those of a child. She had been living alone with her mother, a Jew of Polish origin, in a street in the Goutte-d'Or district, the Rue de Chartres, no distance from the Rue Polonceau where Cécile, Ernest, and Dora Bruder had lived. To avoid dying of starvation, the mother worked night shifts in a workshop that made mittens for the Wehrmacht. The daughter went to school in the Rue Jean-François-Lépine. At the end of 1942, because of the roundups, the headmistress had advised the mother to send her child into hiding, and it was doubtless she who had given her the address of the Saint-Coeur-de-Marie.

To disguise her origins, she was enrolled at the boarding school under the name of "Suzanne Albert." Shortly afterward, she fell ill. She was sent to the infirmary. There, she saw a doctor. After a while, since she refused to eat, it was decided to send her home.

She remembers everything in that boarding school as being black—walls, classrooms, infirmary—except for the white coifs of the nuns. It seemed more like an orphanage. Iron discipline. No heating. Nothing to eat but root vegetables. Boarders' prayers took place at "six o'clock," and I forgot to ask her whether she meant six in the morning or six at night.

. . . .

Dora spent the summer of 1940 at the boarding school. On Sundays, she would certainly have gone to visit her parents, who were still living in the hotel room at 41 Boulevard Ornano. I look at the plan of the métro and try to retrace her route in my mind. The simplest, avoiding too many changes, is to take a train from Nation, a station fairly near the boarding school. Pont-de-Sèvres line. Change at Strasbourg-Saint-Denis. Porte de Clignancourt line. She would have got out at Simplon, just opposite the cinema and the hotel.

Twenty years later, I often took the métro at Simplon. It was always about ten o'clock at night. At that hour, the station was deserted, and there were long intervals between trains.

Late on Sunday afternoons, she too would have returned by the same route. Did her parents go with her? Once at Nation, she had to walk, and the quickest way to the Rue de Picpus was via the Rue Fabre-d'Églantine.

It was like going back to prison. The days were drawing in. It was already dark when she crossed the courtyard, passing the funerary monument with its imitation grotto. Above the steps, a single lamp was lit over the door. She followed the corridors. Chapel, for Sunday evening Benediction. Then, into line, in silence as far as the dormitory.

....

AUTUMN HAD COME. ON 2 OCTOBER, THE PARIS NEWS-papers published the decree obliging all Jews to register at police stations for a census. A declaration by the head of the family sufficed for all. To avoid long lines, those affected were asked to attend in alphabetical order, on the dates indicated in the table below . . .

The letter B fell on 4 October. On that day, Ernest Bruder went to Clignancourt police station to fill in the census form. But he failed to register his daughter. Everybody reporting for the census was allotted a number, later attached to the "family file." This was known as the "Jewish dossier" number.

Ernest and Cécile Bruder had the Jewish dossier number 49091. But Dora had no number of any sort.

Perhaps Ernest Bruder felt that she was out of harm's way, in a free zone, at the Saint-Coeur-de-Marie boarding school, and that it was best not to draw attention to her. Then again, the classification "Jew" meant nothing to the fourteen-year-old Dora. When it came down to it, what exactly did the Bruders understand by the term "Jew"? For himself, he never gave it a thought. He was used to being put into this or that category by the authorities and accepted it without question. Unskilled laborer. Ex-Austrian. French legionnaire. Non-suspect. Ex-serviceman 100% disabled. Foreign statute laborer. Jew. And the same went for his wife, Cécile. Ex-Austrian. Non-suspect. Furrier's seamstress. Jewess. As yet, the only person who had escaped all classification, including the number 49091, was Dora.

Who knows, she might have escaped to the end. She had only to remain within the boarding school's dark walls and merge into their shadows; and, by scrupulously observing its daily and nightly routine, avoid drawing attention to herself. Dormitory. Chapel. Refectory. Playground. Classroom. Chapel. Dormitory.

It chanced—but was it really chance—that, at the Saint-Coeur-de-Marie boarding school, she was back within sight of her birthplace on the opposite side of the street. 15 Rue Santerre. The Rothschild Hospital maternity ward. Rue Santerre was a continuation of the Rue de la Gare-de-Reuilly and thus ran alongside the school wall.

A quiet, tree-shaded neighborhood. When, twenty-five years ago, in June 1971, I spent an entire day walking around there, I found it unchanged. Occasionally, a summer shower obliged me to take shelter in an archway. That afternoon, without knowing why, I had the impression of walking in another's footsteps.

After the summer of '42, the area around the Saint-Coeur-de-Marie became particularly dangerous. For two years there had been a succession of roundups, at the Rothschild Hospital, at its orphanage of the same name, Rue Lamblardie, and at the hospice, 76 Rue de Picpus, where the Gaspard Meyer who had signed Dora's birth certificate lived and worked. The Rothschild Hospital was a trap for the sick from Drancy camp, sent there only to be returned to the camp whenever it suited the Germans, who were keeping watch on 15 Rue Santerre with the help of a private police agency, the Agence Faralicq. A great many children and adolescents of Dora's age were arrested, taken from their hiding place in the Rothschild Orphanage, Rue Lamblardie, the first street on the right after the Rue de la Gare-de-Reuilly. And, on the Rue de la Gare-de-Reuilly itself, at number 48*bis,* exactly opposite the boarding school wall, nine boys and girls of Dora's age or, in some cases, younger, were arrested with their families. Indeed, the garden and courtyard of the Saint-Coeur-de-Marie boarding school were the sole enclave in this entire block of houses to remain inviolate. But only on condition that you never went out, that you stayed forgotten within the shadow of those dark walls, themselves engulfed by the darkness of the curfew.

I'm writing these pages in November 1996. It seldom stops raining. Tomorrow we shall be in December, and fifty-five years will have passed since Dora ran away. It gets dark early, and it's just as well: night obliterates the grayness and monotony of these rainy days when you wonder if it really is daytime, or if we are going through some intermediary stage, a sort of gloomy eclipse lasting till dusk. Then the street lamps and shop windows and cafés light up, the evening air freshens, contours sharpen, there are traffic jams at the crossroads and hurrying crowds in the streets. And in the midst of all these lights, all this hubbub, I can hardly believe that this is the city where Dora lived with her parents, where my father lived when he was twenty years younger than I am now. I feel as though I am alone in making the link between Paris then and Paris now, alone in remembering all these details. There are moments when the link is strained and in danger of snapping, and other evenings when the city of yesterday appears to me in fleeting gleams behind that of today.

I've been rereading the fifth and sixth volumes of *Les Misérables*. Victor Hugo describes Cosette and Jean Valjean, tracked by Javert, making their way across Paris, by night, from the Barrière Saint-Jacques to the Petit Picpus. You can follow part of their itinerary on a map. They are near the Seine. Cosette begins to tire. Jean Valjean carries her in his arms. Taking the back streets, they skirt the Jardin des Plantes and come to the riverbank. They cross the Pont d'Austerlitz. Scarcely has Jean Valjean set foot on the right bank than he thinks he sees shadowy figures on the bridge. Their only means of escape—he tells himself—is to take the little Rue du Chemin-Vert-Saint-Antoine.

And suddenly, you have a sensation of vertigo, as if Cosette and Jean Valjean, to escape Javert and his police, have taken a leap into space: thus far, they have been following real Paris streets, and now, abruptly, Victor Hugo thrusts them into the imaginary district of Paris that he calls the Petit Picpus. It is the same sense of strangeness that overcomes you when you find yourself walking through an unfamiliar district in a dream. On waking, you realize, little by little, that the pattern of its streets had overlaid the one with which, in daytime, you are familiar.

And here is what disturbs me: at the end of their flight across a district whose topography and street names had been invented by Victor Hugo, Cosette and Jean Valjean just manage to escape a police patrol by slipping behind a wall. They find themselves in "a sort of garden, very large and of singular appearance; one of those gloomy gardens which seem to be made to be seen in the winter and at night." This garden where the pair hide is that of a convent, which Victor Hugo situates precisely at number 62 Rue du Petit-Picpus, the same address as that of the Saint-Coeur-de-Marie school where Dora was a boarder.

"At the period to which this history relates," Victor Hugo writes, "a boarding-school was attached to the convent. . . . These young girls . . . were dressed in blue with a white cap. . . . There were in the inclosure of the Petit Picpus three perfectly distinct buildings, the Great Convent, in which the nuns lived, the school building, in which the pupils lodged, and finally what was called the Little Convent."

And, having given a minute description of the place, he continues: "We could not pass by this extraordinary, unknown, obscure house without entering and leading in those who accompany us, and who listen as we relate, for the benefit of some, perhaps, the melancholy history of Jean Valjean."

Like many writers before me, I believe in coincidence and, sometimes, in the novelist's gift for clairvoyance—the word "gift" not being the exact term, for it implies a kind of superiority. No, it simply comes with the profession: the imaginative leaps this requires, the need to fix your mind on points of detail—to the point of obsession, in fact—so as not to lose the thread and give in to natural laziness—all this tension, this cerebral exercise may well lead in the long run to "flashes of intuition concerning events past and future," as the Larousse dictionary puts it, under the heading "clairvoyance."

In December 1988, after reading the notice about the search for Dora in the *Paris-Soir* of December 1941, I thought about it incessantly for months. The precision of certain details haunted me: "41 Boulevard Ornano, 1 m 55, oval-shaped face, gray-brown eyes, gray sports jacket, maroon pullover, navy blue skirt and hat, brown gym shoes." And all enveloped in night, ignorance, forgetfulness, oblivion. It seemed to me that I should never succeed in finding the faintest trace of Dora Bruder. At the time, the emptiness I felt prompted me to write a novel, *Voyage de noces,* it being as good a way as any of continuing to fix my attention on Dora Bruder, and perhaps, I told myself, of elucidating or divining something about her, a place where she had been, a detail of her life. When it came to her parents, and the circumstances of her escape, I was completely ignorant. All I had to go on was this: I had seen her name, BRUDER DORA—nothing else, no date or place of birth—above that of her father—BRUDER ERNEST, *21.5.99, Vienna. Stateless.*—on the list of those dispatched on the transport that had left on 18 September 1942 for Auschwitz.

I was thinking, when writing *Voyage de noces,* of certain women whom I knew in the sixties, women like Anne B., Bella D.—the same age as Dora, one of them almost to the month—who, during the Occupation, were in the same situation and might have shared her fate, and whom she probably resembled. Today, it occurs to me that I had had to write two hundred pages before I captured, unconsciously, a vague gleam of the truth.

It was a matter of a few words: "The terminus was Nation. Rigaud and Ingrid had allowed Bastille, the stop where they should have changed for Porte Dorée, to go by. Emerging from the exit, they were confronted by a vast expanse of snow. . . . The sleigh cut through the back streets to reach the Boulevard Soult."

These back streets lay behind the Rue de Picpus and the Saint-Coeur-de-Marie boarding school from which Dora Bruder made her escape, one December evening when it was probably snowing in Paris.

That was the only moment in the book when, without knowing it, I came close to her in space and time.

THUS WE FIND NEXT TO DORA BRUDER'S NAME IN THE school register, under the heading "Date and reason for departure": "14 December 1941. Pupil has run away."

It was a Sunday. I imagine that she would have taken advantage of the free day to visit her parents. That evening, she failed to return to the school.

Those dying weeks of the year were the blackest, most claustrophobic period that Paris had experienced since the beginning of the Occupation. Between 8 and 14 December, in reprisal for two assassination attempts, the Germans ordered a curfew from six o'clock in the evening. Next came the roundup of seven hundred French Jews on 12 December; and the fine of one billion francs levied on the Jewish community as a whole. And then, on the morning of the same day, the shooting of seventy hostages at the Mont-Valérien fortress. On 10 December, by order of the Prefect of Police, French and foreign Jews living in the department of the Seine had to submit to "periodic checks," producing special identity cards stamped "Jew" or "Jewess." Henceforth they were forbidden to travel outside the department, and any change of address had to be registered at a police station.

In the 18th arrondissement, a curfew imposed by the Germans had been in force since 1 December. Nobody could enter the area after six o'clock at night. Local métro stations were closed, including Simplon, the one nearest to where Ernest and Cécile Bruder lived. A hand grenade had been thrown in the Rue Championnet, very close to their hotel.

The curfew lasted three days. No sooner had it been lifted than the Germans imposed another throughout the entire 10th arrondissement, where, on the Boulevard Magenta, persons unknown had fired at an officer of the occupying authorities. Then came the general curfew of 8 to 14 December—the Sunday of Dora's escape.

Around the Saint-Coeur-de-Marie boarding school, as the lights were extinguished in district after district, the city became a dark prison. While Dora was behind the high walls of 60–62 Rue de Picpus, her parents were confined to their hotel room.

Her father having failed to declare her a "Jewess" in October 1940, she had not been allotted a "Jewish dossier" number. But the decree issued by the Prefecture of Police on 10 December, pertaining to the control of Jews, had stipulated that "subsequent changes in the family situation must be reported." I doubt if Dora's father would have had either the time or the inclination to get her inscribed on a file before her escape. He must have thought that the Prefecture of Police would never suspect her existence while she remained at the Saint-Coeur-de-Marie.

What makes us decide to run away? I remember my own flight on 18 January 1960, at a period that had none of the blackness of December 1941. Along my escape route, past the hangars of Villacoublay airfield, the only point I had in common with Dora was the season: winter. A calm, ordinary winter, not to be compared with the winter of eighteen years earlier. But it seems that the sudden urge to escape can be prompted by one of those cold, gray days that makes you more than ever aware of your solitude and intensifies your feeling that a trap is about to close.

Sunday 14 December was the first day that the curfew had been lifted for almost a week. People were now free to go out after six o'clock in the evening. But because of German Time,[1] darkness fell in the afternoon.

At what moment of the day did the Sisters of Divine Mercy first notice that Dora was missing? It is certain to have been evening. Perhaps after Benediction in the chapel, as the boarders went up to the dormitory. I expect the Mother Superior tried to reach Dora's parents at once, to find out if she had stayed with them. Did she know that Dora and her parents were Jewish? According to her biographical note, "Many children from the families of persecuted Jews found refuge in the Saint-Coeur-de-Marie, thanks to the courageous and charitable actions of Sister Marie-Jean-Baptiste. Supported in this by the discreet and no less courageous attitude of her nuns, she shrank from nothing, whatever the risk."

But Dora's was a special case. In May 1940, when she entered the Saint-Coeur-de-Marie, the persecutions had not yet begun. She had missed the census in October 1940. And it was

---

1. The occupying authorities had brought the clocks forward by one hour to correspond with German Reich time.

not till July 1942, after the great roundup, that religious institutions began to hide Jewish children. She had been at the Saint-Coeur-de-Marie for a year and a half. In all likelihood, she was its sole Jewish pupil. Was this common knowledge among the nuns, among her fellow boarders?

The Café Marchal on the ground floor of the hotel at 41 Boulevard Ornano had a telephone: Montmartre 44–74; but I don't know if it had a line to the hotel, or if that, too, was owned by Marchal. The Saint-Coeur-de-Marie boarding school is not listed in the telephone directory for the period. I've found a separate address for the Sisters of the Christian Schools of Divine Mercy, but in 1942 this must have been an annex to the boarding school: 64 Rue Saint-Maur. Did Dora go there? It too had no telephone number.

Who knows? The Mother Superior may have waited till Monday morning before telephoning the Café Marchal or, as is more likely, sending a nun to 41 Boulevard Ornano. Unless Cécile and Ernest Bruder went to the boarding school themselves.

It would help to know if the weather was fine on 14 December, the day of Dora's escape. Perhaps it was one of those mild, sunny winter days when you have a feeling of holiday and eternity—the illusory feeling that the course of time is suspended, and that you need only slip through this breach to escape the trap that is closing around you.

F OR A LONG TIME, AFTER HER ESCAPE AND THE NOTICE about the search for her that was printed in *Paris-Soir,* I knew nothing about Dora Bruder. Then I learned that, eight months later, on 13 August 1942, she had been interned in the camp at Drancy. The dossier showed that she had come from Tourelles camp. On that very 13 August, indeed, three hundred Jewish women were transferred from Tourelles to Drancy.

Tourelles prison "camp," or rather internment center, occupied former colonial infantry barracks at 11 Boulevard Mortier, near the Porte des Lilas. It had been opened in October 1940 for the internment of foreign Jews whose situation was deemed "irregular." But after 1941, while men were sent directly to Drancy, or to camps in the Loiret, only Jewish women who contravened German regulations were to be interned in Tourelles, together with women who were Communists or common criminals.

When, and for what precise reasons, was Dora Bruder sent to Tourelles? I thought there might have been a document, a clue, to provide me with the answer. I was reduced to making assumptions. She was probably stopped in the street. In February 1942—two months after her escape—the Germans had issued a decree forbidding Jews to change address or leave home after eight o'clock at night. Surveillance in the streets thus became stricter than in preceding months. Eventually, I came to the conclusion that Dora was captured during that dismal, icy-cold February when the Jewish Affairs police[1] set their ambushes in the corridors of the métro, at the entrances to cinemas, the exits of theaters. In fact, it astonished me that a sixteen-year-old girl, whose description and disappearance in December were known to the police, had managed to elude her captors for so long. Unless she had found a hideout. But where, in that Paris winter of 1941–42, the darkest and most severe of the Occupation, with snow from November onward, a temperature of −15° C in January, frozen puddles and black ice everywhere and renewed heavy snowfalls in February? So what refuge could she have found? And how did she manage to survive in a Paris like that?

It would have been February, I imagine, when "they" had caught her in their net. "They" could as easily have been uniformed men on the beat as inspectors from either the Brigade for the Protection of Minors[2] or the Jewish Affairs police carrying out an identity check in a public place . . . I had read in a book of memoirs that girls of eighteen or nineteen, and even some as young as sixteen, Dora's age, had been sent to Tourelles for trivial infringements of "German decrees." That same February, on the evening when the German decrees came into force, my father was caught in a roundup on the Champs-Élysées. Inspectors of the Jewish Affairs police had blocked the exits of a restaurant in the Rue de Marignan where he was dining with a girlfriend. They asked everybody for their papers.

---

1. The Police aux Questions Juives (PQJ), established November 1941.
2. Brigade des mineurs.

My father carried none. He was arrested. In the Black Maria[3] taking them from the Champs-Élysées to PQJ headquarters in the Rue Greffulhe, he noticed, among other shadowy figures, a young girl of about eighteen. He lost sight of her as they were being hustled up to the floor of this police den where its chief, a certain Superintendent Schweblin, had his office. Then, taking advantage of a light on a time switch that went out just as he was being escorted downstairs to be taken to the Dépôt,[4] he succeeded in making his escape.

My father had barely mentioned this young girl when telling me about his narrow escape for the first and only time in his life, one night in June 1953, in a restaurant off the Champs-Élysées almost opposite the one where he was arrested twenty years before. He had given me no details of her looks, of her clothes. I had all but forgotten her until the day that I learned of Dora Bruder's existence. Then suddenly the memory of her presence among the other unknowns who were with my father in the Black Maria on that February night resurfaced in my mind, and it occurred to me that she might have been Dora Bruder, that she too had just been arrested and was about to be sent to Tourelles.

Perhaps it was that I wanted them to have met, she and my father, in that winter of 1942. Utterly different though they were, one from the other, both, that winter, had been classed

---

3. The French phrase is *panier à salade*, a colloquial term for the police van with an open wire cage that resembles a salad-washing basket.
4. A holding center in the Prefecture of Police.

51

in the same category, as outlaws. My father, too, had missed the census in October 1940 and, like Dora Bruder, had no "Jewish dossier" number. Consequently, no longer having any legal existence, he had cut all threads with a world where you were nothing without a job, a family, a nationality, a date of birth, an address. Henceforth he was in limbo. Not unlike Dora, after her escape.

But on reflection, their respective fates were very different. There were few courses open to a sixteen-year-old girl left to fend for herself, in Paris, in the winter of 1942, after having escaped from a boarding school. In the eyes of the police and the authorities of the day, her situation was doubly "irregular": she was not only Jewish, she was a juvenile on the run.

As for my father, who was fourteen years older than Dora Bruder, the way was already mapped out: since they had made him into an outlaw, he had no choice but to follow that same course, to live on his wits in Paris and vanish into the swamps of the black market.

Not so long ago, I discovered that the girl in the Black Maria could not have been Dora Bruder. I was looking for her name on the list of women who had been interned in Tourelles camp. Of these, two, Polish Jews aged twenty and twenty-one, had entered Tourelles on 18 and 19 February 1942. Their names were Syma Berger and Fredel Traister. The dates fitted, but was she in fact either girl? After passing through the Dépôt, men were sent to the camp at Drancy, women to Tourelles. Perhaps, like my father, the unknown girl had escaped the common fate in store for them. I believe that she will always remain anonymous, like all those shadowy figures arrested that night. The Jewish Affairs police having destroyed their files, there are no records of arrests made during a roundup, nor of individuals picked up on the street. Were I not here to record it, there would be no trace of this unidentified girl's presence, nor that of my father's, in a Black Maria on the Champs-Élysées in February 1942. Nothing but those individuals—living or dead—officially classed as "person unknown."

Twenty years later, my mother was acting in a play at the Théâtre Michel. Often, I would wait for her in a café on the corner of the Rue des Mathurins and the Rue Greffulhe. I didn't know then that my father had risked his life near there, or that I had entered a zone that was once a black hole. We would dine in a restaurant on the Rue Greffulhe—perhaps on the ground floor of the PQJ building where my father had been hustled into Superintendent Schweblin's office. Jacques Schweblin. Born 1901, Mulhouse. It was his men, at the camps of Drancy and Pithiviers, who eagerly undertook the search of internees prior to each departure for Auschwitz:

> M. Schweblin, head of the PQJ, would arrive at the
> camp accompanied by 5 or 6 aides whom he identified as
> "auxiliaries," giving nobody's name but his own. Each of
> these plainclothes policemen wore a uniform belt with a
> pistol hanging from one side and a nightstick from the
> other.
> Once he had installed his aides, M. Schweblin left the

camp, returning only in the evening to collect the fruits of their search. Each aide would set himself up in a hut containing a table and, beside it, two receptacles, one for cash, the other for jewelry. The internees then filed past the men, who proceeded to subject them to a minute and humiliating search. Very often they were beaten or forced to remove their trousers and submit to a hard kicking, accompanied by remarks like "Hey you! Want another taste of the police boot?" Frequently, on the pretext of expediting the search, inside and outside pockets were torn. I will pass over the intimate body searches suffered by the women.

Once the search was over, cash and jewelry were piled anyhow into boxes that were bound with string and sealed before being loaded into M. Schweblin's car.

This process was a farce, given that the sealing tongs were in the hands of the policemen, who were free to help themselves to banknotes and jewels. In fact, these men would openly produce a valuable ring from their pockets, saying "Hey, that's not bad!," or a fistful of 1,000- or 500-franc notes, saying "Hey, I forgot this." Bedding in the huts was also searched: mattresses, eiderdowns, and bolsters were torn apart. Of all the many searches performed by the Jewish Affairs police, not a single trace remains.[5]

---

5. Extract from an official report drawn up in November 1943 by a manager from Pithiviers Tax Office.

The search team always consisted of the same seven men. Plus one woman. Their names are unknown. They were young at the time, so some must still be alive today. But their faces would be unrecognizable.

Schweblin disappeared in 1943. The Germans disposed of him themselves. Yet when my father was telling me about being taken to this man's office, he said that he was positive that he had recognized him at the Porte Maillot, one Sunday after the war.

BLACK MARIAS REMAINED MUCH THE SAME TILL THE early sixties. The only time I ever found myself in one it was with my father, and I wouldn't mention it now had not this episode taken on a symbolic character in my eyes.

The circumstances were banal in the extreme. I was eighteen years old, still a minor. My parents, though separated, still lived in the same block, my father with a woman who had yellow hair the color of straw and was very high-strung, a sort of imitation Mylène Demongeot. And I with my mother. That day, on the landing, a quarrel had broken out between my parents about the very modest sum that my father had been ordered to pay for my support following a series of judicial proceedings: High Court of the Seine. 1st Auxiliary Chamber, Court of Appeals Notification of Judgment. My mother wished me to ring at his door and demand this money, which he hadn't paid. It was, alas, all we had to live on. Grumbling, I did as I was told. I rang my father's bell meaning to ask him nicely, even to apologize for bothering him. He slammed the door in my face; I could hear the pseudo Mylène Demongeot on the telephone to the police emergency service, screaming something about "a hooligan making trouble."

They came for me at my mother's about ten minutes later, and my father and I climbed into the waiting Black Maria. We sat facing one another, on wooden benches, each flanked by two policemen. I thought to myself that if it was the first time in my life that something like this had happened to me, my father had been through it all before, on that February night twenty years ago when the Jewish Affairs police had taken him away in a Black Maria much like this one. And I wondered if, at that moment, he was thinking the same thing. But he avoided my gaze, pretending not to see me.

I remember every minute of that drive. The embankments along the Seine. The Rue des Saint-Pères. The Boulevard Saint-Germain. The stop at the lights opposite the terrace of the Café des Deux-Magots. I peered enviously through the barred windows at the drinkers sitting on the terrace in the sun. Luckily, I had little to worry about: we were in that anodyne, innocuous period later known as the "Thirty Glorious Years."[1]

Yet I was surprised that, after all he had been through during the Occupation, my father should have offered not the slightest objection to my being taken away in a Black Maria. Sitting there, opposite me, impassive, with an air of faint disgust, he ignored me as if I had the plague, and, knowing that I could expect no sympathy from him, I dreaded our arrival at the police station. And I felt the injustice of this all the more since I had embarked on a book—my first—in which, putting myself in his shoes, I relived his feelings of distress during the Occupation. A few years earlier, among his books, I had come across certain anti-Semitic works from the forties, books that he must have bought at the time in an effort to understand

---

1. "Les Trentes Glorieuses," the postwar boom in France.

what it was that these writers had against him. And I can well imagine his surprise at the portrayal of this imaginary, phantasmagoric monster with clawlike hands and hooked nose whose shadow flitted across the walls, this creature corrupted by every vice, responsible for every evil, guilty of every crime. As for me, I wanted my first book to be a riposte to all those who, by insulting my father, had wounded me. And, on the terrain of French prose, to silence them once and for all. I can see now that my plan was childishly naive: most of the authors had disappeared, executed by firing squad, exiled, far gone in senility, or dead of old age. Yes, alas, I was too late.

The Black Maria drew up in the Rue de l'Abbaye outside Saint-Germain police station. Our guards led us into the superintendent's office. Crisply, my father explained to him that I was a "hooligan" who had been "giving trouble" since I was sixteen years old. The superintendent declared—addressing me in the tone you use to a delinquent—that he would keep me in, "if there's a next time." I had the distinct impression that if the superintendent had carried out his threat and sent me to the Dépôt, my father wouldn't have lifted a finger to help me.

My father and I left the police station together. I asked him if it was really necessary to call the emergency service and "charge" me in front of our guards. He didn't answer. I bore him no grudge. Since we lived in the same building, we set off home side by side, in silence. I was tempted to remind him of that night in February 1942 when he too had been taken away in a Black Maria, to ask him whether he had been thinking of that, just now. But perhaps it meant less to him than it did to me.

On the way back, we didn't exchange a single word, not even when we parted on the stairs. I was to see him once or twice in August of the following year, on an occasion when he hid my call-up papers as a ruse to have me carted off by force to the Reuilly army barracks. I never saw him again after that.

....

WHAT DID DORA BRUDER DO FIRST, I WONDER, AS soon as she had made her escape on 14 December 1941. Perhaps she had decided not to return to the boarding school the instant she had arrived at the gate, and had spent the evening wandering the streets till curfew.

Streets that still had countrified names: Les Meuniers, La Bèche-aux-Loups, Le Sentier des Merisiers. But at the top of the little tree-shaded street that ran alongside the perimeter wall of the Saint-Coeur-de-Marie there was a freight depot, and further on, if you take the Avenue Daumesnil, the Gare de Lyon. The railway lines to this station pass within a few hundred meters of the school where Dora Bruder had been shut up. This peaceful quarter, seemingly remote from Paris, with its convents, its hidden cemeteries and quiet avenues, is also a point of departure.

I don't know if the proximity of the Gare de Lyon encouraged Dora to run away. Whether from her dormitory in the silence of the blackout, she could hear the rumble of freight cars or the sound of trains leaving the Gare de Lyon for the Free Zone . . . She was doubtless familiar with those two duplicitous words: Free Zone.

In the novel I had written at a time when I knew almost nothing about Dora Bruder but wanted to keep her in the forefront of my mind, the girl of her age whom I called Ingrid hides in the Free Zone with her boyfriend. I was thinking of

Bella D. who, at the age of fifteen, had smuggled herself out of Paris across the demarcation line, only to end up in a Toulouse prison; of Anne B., who was picked up without a travel permit on Chalon-sur-Saône station and sentenced to twelve weeks in prison . . . These are things that they had told me about in the sixties.

Did Dora Bruder prepare for her escape long in advance, with the complicity of a friend, boy or girl? Did she remain in Paris, or did she in fact try to reach the Free Zone?

. . . .

THE POLICE BLOTTER AT THE CLIGNANCOURT STATION
has this entry for 27 December 1941 under columns
headed *Date and subject. Marital status. Summary:*

> 27 December 1941. Bruder Dora, born Paris 12th,
> 25/2/26, domiciled at 41 Boulevard Ornano. Interview
> with Bruder Ernest, age 42, father.

The following figures are written in the margin, but I have
no idea what they stand for: 7029 21/12.

The superintendent at Clignancourt police station, 12 Rue
Lambert, behind the Butte Montmartre, was called Siri. But
Ernest Bruder probably went to the divisional station, 74 Rue
du Mont-Cenis, next to the town hall, which was also part of
the Clignancourt district: it was nearer his home. The superintendent there was called Cornec.

Dora had run away thirteen days earlier, and Ernest Bruder
had waited all that time before notifying the police of his
daughter's disappearance. His anguish and indecision during
those long thirteen days can be imagined. During the census
of October 1940, he had omitted to register Dora at this very
police station, and they were bound to notice. By trying to find
her, he was drawing attention to her.

The transcript of Ernest Bruder's interview is missing from
the Prefecture of Police archives. No doubt local police stations destroy documents of that kind as they become obso-

lete. A few years after the war, other police records were destroyed, such as the special registers opened during the week in June 1942 when every Jewish person over the age of six was issued with three yellow stars. These registers, which had a column in the margin where you signed on receipt of your stars, recorded your civil status, identity card number, and domicile. Police stations in Paris and the suburbs compiled over fifty such registers.

We shall never know how Ernest Bruder answered the questions put to him about his daughter and himself. Perhaps he chanced on a desk clerk for whom it was a matter of routine, like before the war, and who saw no particular difference between Ernest Bruder and his daughter and any other French citizen. To be sure, the man was an "ex-Austrian," and an unskilled laborer living in a hotel. But his daughter was born in Paris and had French nationality. A runaway adolescent. It happens more and more in these troubled times. Did this policeman advise Ernest Bruder to put the missing notice in *Paris-Soir,* given that almost two weeks had passed since Dora's disappearance? Or did a *Paris-Soir* reporter, touring the police stations in search of "filler," happen to see it among other incidents of the day and glean it for the paper's "From Day to Day" columns?

I remember the intensity of my feelings while I was on the run in January 1960—an intensity such as I have seldom known. It was the intoxication of cutting all ties at a stroke: the clean break, deliberately made, from enforced rules, boarding school, teachers, classmates; you have nothing to do with these people from now on; the break from your parents, who have never understood you, and from whom, you tell yourself, it's useless to expect any help; feelings of rebellion and solitude carried to flash point, taking your breath away and leaving you in a state of weightlessness. It was probably one of the few times in my life when I was truly myself and following my own bent.

This ecstasy cannot last. It has no future. You are swiftly brought down to earth.

Running away—it seems—is a call for help and occasionally a form of suicide. At least you experience a moment of eternity. You have broken your ties not only with the world but also with time. And one fine morning you find that the sky is a pale blue and that nothing now weighs you down. In the Tuileries garden, the hands on the clock have stopped for good. An ant is transfixed in its journey across a patch of sunlight.

I think of Dora Bruder. I remind myself that, for her, running away was not as easy as it was for me, twenty years later, in a world that had once more been made safe. To her, everything in that city of December 1941, its curfews, its soldiers, its police, was hostile, intent on her destruction. At sixteen years old, without knowing why, she had the entire world against her.

Other rebels, in the Paris of those years, equally solitary, were throwing hand grenades at the Germans, into their conveys and meetings. They were her age. Some of their faces appeared on the *Affiche Rouge*,[1] and, despite myself, I keep associating them in my mind with Dora.

In the summer of 1941, one of the films made under the Occupation, first shown in Normandy, came to the local Paris cinemas. It was a harmless comedy: *Premier rendez-vous*. The last time I saw it, I had a strange feeling, out of keeping with the thin plot and the sprightly tones of the actors. I told myself that perhaps, one Sunday, Dora Bruder had been to see this film, the subject of which was a girl of her age who runs away. She escapes from a boarding school much like the Saint-Coeur-de-Marie. During her flight, as in fairy tales and romances, she meets her Prince Charming.

This film paints a rosy, anodyne picture of what had happened to Dora in real life. Did it give her the idea of running away? I concentrated on details: the dormitory, the school corridors, the boarders' uniforms, the café where the heroine waits after dark . . . I could find nothing that might correspond to the reality, and in any case most of the scenes were shot in the studio. And yet, I had a sense of unease. It stemmed from the film's peculiar luminosity, from the grain of the actual stock. Every image seemed veiled in an arctic whiteness that accentuated the contrasts and sometimes obliterated them. The lighting was at once too bright and too dim, either stifling the voices or making their timbre louder, more disturbing.

---

1. "Wanted" posters printed in red, put up by the Germans.

Suddenly, I realized that this film was impregnated with the gaze of moviegoers from the time of the Occupation— people from all walks of life, most of whom would not have survived the war. They had been taken out of themselves after having seen this film one Saturday night, their night out. While it lasted, you forgot the war and the menacing world outside. Huddled together in the dark of a cinema, you were caught up in the flow of images on the screen, and nothing more could happen to you. And, by some kind of chemical process, this combined gaze had materially altered the actual film, the lighting, the voices of the actors. That is what I had sensed, thinking of Dora Bruder and faced with the ostensibly trivial images of *Premier rendez-vous.*

. . . .

ERNEST BRUDER WAS ARRESTED ON 19 MARCH 1942, or rather, that was the day he was interned at Drancy. I've been unable to find any trace of the circumstances of his arrest, nor of the reasons for it. In what was called a "family file," where data on each individual Jew were assembled for use at the Prefecture of Police, his entry reads:

Bruder Ernest
21.5.99—Vienna
Jewish dossier no.: 49091
Trade or profession: None
French legionnaire, 2d class. 100% disabled. Gassed;
    pulmonary tuberculosis
Central police register E56404

Lower down, the file has been stamped WANTED, next to which somebody has penciled the words: "Traced to Drancy camp."

As a Jew and an "ex-Austrian," Ernest Bruder could have been arrested in the roundup of August 1941, during which the French police, backed by the German army, had cordoned off the 11th arrondissement on 20 August and then, in the days that followed, stopped and questioned foreign Jews in the streets of other arrondissements, including the 18th. How had he escaped this roundup? Thanks to his rank as an ex-French legionnaire, 2d class? I doubt it.

Evidently, from his file, he was "wanted." But since when? And why, exactly? If he was already "wanted" on 27 December 1941, the day he had notified the Clignancourt police of Dora's disappearance, he wouldn't have been allowed to leave the police station. Did he draw attention to himself on that day?

A father tries to find his daughter, reports her disappearance at a police station, and a wanted notice is inserted in an evening newspaper. But the father himself is "wanted." Parents lose all trace of their daughter and, one 19 March, one of them disappears in his turn, as if the winter that year was cutting people off from one another, muddying and wiping out their tracks to the point where their existence is in doubt. And there is no redress. The very people whose job it is to search for you are themselves compiling dossiers, the better to ensure that, once found, you will disappear again—this time for good.

. . . .

I DON'T KNOW WHETHER OR NOT DORA BRUDER LEARNED of her father's arrest at once. I imagine not. By March, she had still not returned to 41 Boulevard Ornano after her escape in December. Or so it would seem from such traces of her as survive in the archives of the Prefecture of Police.

Now that almost sixty years have passed, these archives will gradually reveal their secrets. All that remains of the building occupied by the Prefecture of Police during the Occupation is a huge spectral barracks beside the Seine. Whenever we evoke the past, it reminds us a little of the House of Usher. And we can hardly believe that this building we pass every day can be unchanged since the forties. We persuade ourselves that these cannot be the same stones, the same corridors.

The superintendents and inspectors who hunted down the Jews are long dead, and their names echo with a sombre ring and give off a smell of rotting leather and stale tobacco: Permilleux, François, Schweblin, Koerperich, Cougoule . . . Also dead, or far gone in senility, are the street police, known to us as the "press-gang," who signed the transcript of every interview with those whom they arrested during the roundups. Every one of those tens of thousands of transcripts was destroyed, and we shall never know the identity of the members of the "press-gang." But there remain, in the archives, hundreds and hundreds of letters addressed to the Prefect of Police of the day, and to which he never replied. They have been there for over half a century, like sacks of airmail lying forgotten in the recesses of a remote hangar. Now we can read them. Those to whom they were addressed having ignored them, it is we, who were not even born at the time, who are their recipients and their guardians.

TO THE PREFECT OF POLICE
SIR,

I humbly draw your attention to my request. It concerns my nephew Albert Graudens, of French nationality, aged sixteen, who had been interned at . . .

TO THE DIRECTOR OF THE POLICE FOR JEWISH AFFAIRS
SIR,

I implore you to have the great kindness to release my daughter, Nelly Trautmann, from Drancy camp . . .

TO THE PREFECT OF POLICE
SIR,

I venture to ask you a favor in respect of my husband, Zelik Pergricht, so that I may know where he is and have a little news . . .

TO THE PREFECT OF POLICE
SIR,

I humbly beg you in your great kindness and generosity for news of my daughter, Mme Jacques Lévy, née Violette Joël, arrested about 10 September last as she was trying to cross the demarcation line without wearing the regulation

star. She was accompanied by her son, Jean Lévy, aged
eight and a half . . .

Forwarded to the Prefect of Police:

I beg you to have the kindness to release my grandson,
Michel Robin, aged three, French-born of a French mother,
who is interned with him at Drancy . . .

TO THE PREFECT OF POLICE
SIR,

I would be infinitely grateful if you would be good
enough to take the following cases into consideration: my
parents, both elderly and in poor health, have just been
arrested as Jews, and my little sister, Marie Grosman, aged
fifteen and a half, a French Jew, holding French identity
card no. 1594936, grade B, and myself, Jeanette Grosman,
also a French Jew, aged nineteen, holding French identity
card no. 924247, grade B, have been left on our own . . .

TO THE DIRECTOR OF THE POLICE FOR JEWISH AFFAIRS.
SIR,

Excuse me if I presume to write to you in person about
this, but my husband was taken away at 4 A.M. on 16 July
1942, and as my little girl was crying, they took her at the
same time.
Her name is Pauline Gothelf, aged fourteen and a half,
born 19 November 1927 in Paris, 12th arrondissement, and
she is French . . .

．．．．．．．．．．．．．．．．．．

F OR THE DATE OF 17 APRIL 1942, THE POLICE BLOTTER
at Clignancourt station has this entry under its usual
headings, *Date and subject. Marital status. Summary:*

> 17 April 1942. 20998 15/24. P. Minors. Case of
> Bruder Dora, age 16, disappeared following Interview
> 1917 has regained maternal domicile.

I don't know what the figures 20998 and 15/24 stand for.
"P. Minors" must mean Protection of Minors. Interview 1917
is certainly the transcript of Ernest Bruder's deposition, and
the questions concerning Dora and himself put to him on 27
December 1941. This is the sole reference in the archives to
Interview 1917.

A bare three lines on the "case of Bruder Dora." The en-
tries that come after it in the blotter for 17 April concern other
"cases":

> Gaul Georgette Paulette, born 30.7.23 Pantin, Seine,
> to Georges and Pelz Rose, spinster, lives in hotel 11 Rue
> Pigalle. Prostitution.
> Germaine Mauraire, born 9.10.21 Entre-Deux-Eaux
> (Vosges). Lives in hotel. 1 P.M. report.[1]

J.-R. CRETET, 9TH ARRONDISSEMENT

---

1. Allusion to a report by the Police des Moeurs, or Vice Squad.

So the list goes on, throughout the Occupation, in the police blotters: prostitutes, lost dogs, abandoned babies. And runaway adolescents—like Dora—guilty of vagrancy.

Apparently, "Jews" as such never came into it. And yet they passed through these same police stations before being taken to the Dépôt, and from there to Drancy. And the phrase "regained maternal domicile" suggests that the Clignancourt police were aware that Dora's father had been arrested the month before.

Of Dora herself, there is no trace between 14 December 1941, the day she ran away, and 17 April 1942 when, in the words of the blotter, she regained the maternal domicile, that is, the hotel room at 41 Boulevard Ornano. For those four months, we have no idea where she went, what she did, whom she was with. Nor do we know the circumstances of her return to the "maternal domicile." Was it of her own accord, after having heard of her father's arrest? Or had she in fact been stopped in the street, the Brigade for the Protection of Minors having issued a warrant for her arrest? So far, I haven't found a single clue, a single witness who might shed light on these four months of absence, for us, a blank in her life.

One way not to lose all touch with Dora Bruder over this period would be to report on the changes in the weather. The first snow fell on 4 November 1941. Winter got off to a cold start on 22 December. On 29 December, the temperature dropped still further, and windowpanes were covered with a thin coating of ice. From 13 January onwards, the cold became Siberian. Water froze. This lasted some four weeks. On

12 February, the sun came out briefly, like a tentative annunciation of spring. The snow on the sidewalks, trampled by pedestrians, turned to a blackish slush. It was on that evening of 12 February that my father was picked up by the Jewish Affairs police. On 22 February it snowed again. On 25 February, there was a fresh, much heavier snowfall. On 3 March, just after 9 P.M., the first bombs fell on the suburbs. Windows rattled in Paris. On 13 March, in broad daylight, the sirens sounded a general alert. Passengers were stuck in the métro for two hours. They were led out through the tunnel. A second alert that same day, at 10 P.M. 15 March was a beautiful sunny day. On 28 March, about 10 P.M., a distant air raid, lasting till midnight. On 2 April, around 4 A.M., an alert, followed by a heavy bombardment till six. More raids from 11 P.M. On 4 April, the buds on the chestnut trees burst open. On 5 April, toward evening, a passing spring storm brought hail and, with it, a rainbow. Don't forget: rendezvous tomorrow afternoon, on the terrace of the Café des Gobelins.

A few months ago, I managed to get hold of a photograph of Dora Bruder, one that is in complete contrast to those already in my collection. It may be the last ever taken of her. Her face and demeanor have none of the childlike qualities that shine out from all the earlier photographs, in the gaze, the rounded cheeks, the white dress worn on a school assembly day . . . I don't know when this photograph was taken. It could only have been in 1941, when Dora was a boarder at the Saint-Coeur-de-Marie, or else early in the spring of 1942, when she returned to the Boulevard Ornano after her escape in December.

She is with her mother and her maternal grandmother. The three women are side by side, the grandmother between Cécile Bruder and Dora. Cécile Bruder wears a black dress, her hair cut short, the grandmother's dress is flowered. Neither woman is smiling. Dora wears a two-piece dress in black—or navy blue—with a white collar, but this could equally well be a cardigan and skirt—the photograph is too dark to see. She wears stockings and ankle-strap shoes. Her midlength hair, held back by a headband, falls almost to her shoulders, her left arm hangs at her side, fingers clenched, her right arm is hidden behind her grandmother. She holds her head high, her eyes are grave, but a smile is beginning to float about her lips. And this gives her face an expression of sad sweetness and defiance. The three women are standing in front of a wall. The ground is paved, as in the passage of some public place. Who could have been the photographer? Ernest Bruder? Or does the fact that he is not present in the photograph mean that he had already been arrested? In any case, it would seem that the three women have put on their Sunday best to face this anonymous lens.

Could it be that Dora is wearing the navy blue skirt mentioned in the missing notice in *Paris-Soir*?

Such photographs exist in every family. They were caught in a few seconds, the duration of the exposure, and these seconds have become an eternity.

Why, I wonder, does the lightning strike in one place rather than another? Suddenly, as I write these lines, I find myself thinking of former colleagues in my profession. Today, I am visited by the memory of a German writer. His name was Friedo Lampe.

It was his name that first caught my attention, and the title of one of his books, *Au bord de la nuit*, translated into French some twenty years ago, at which time I had come across it in a bookshop on the Champs-Élysées. I had never heard of this writer. But even before opening the book, I had divined its tone and atmosphere, as though I had already read him in another life.

Friedo Lampe. *Au bord de la nuit*. For me, name and title evoked those lighted windows from which you cannot tear your gaze. You are persuaded that, behind them, somebody whom you have forgotten has been awaiting your return for years, or else that there is no longer anybody there. Only a lamp, left burning in the empty room.

Friedo Lampe was born in Bremen in 1899, the same year as Ernest Bruder. He had gone to Heidelberg university. He had begun his first novel, *Au bord de la nuit*, in Hamburg, where he worked as a librarian. Later, he took a job with a publisher in Berlin. He took no interest in politics. His passion was for writing about the port of Bremen at nightfall, the lilac-white of the floodlights, the sailors, the wrestlers, the bands, the whistling of the trains, the railway bridge, the siren of a steamship, and all those who seek out their fellow beings at night . . . His novel appeared in October 1933, by which time

Hitler was already in power. *Au bord de la nuit* was withdrawn from the bookshops and pulped, and its author declared "suspect." He was not even Jewish. To what, then, could they possibly object? Quite simply, to the charm and nostalgia of his book. His one ambition—he confided in a letter—was "to bring alive the atmosphere of a port for a few hours in the evening, between eight o'clock and midnight. I'm thinking here of the Bremen district where I grew up. Of short scenes unfolding as in a film, interlocking people's lives. The whole thing light and fluid, linked together very loosely, pictorial, lyric, full of atmosphere."

Toward the end of the war, at the time of the advance of the Russian troops, he was living in a Berlin suburb. On 2 May 1945, he was stopped in the street by two Russian soldiers who asked him for his papers, then dragged him into a garden. And there, without having taken the time to distinguish between the good and the wicked, they beat him to death. Some neighbors buried him nearby, in the shade of a birch tree, and arranged for the police to receive his remains: his papers and his hat.

Like Friedo Lampe, the German writer Felix Hartlaub was a native of the port of Bremen. He was born in 1913. During the Occupation he found himself in Paris. He had a horror of this war, and his uniform the color of verdigris. I know very little about him. In the fifties, a magazine published an extract, in French, from a short book of his, *Von Unten Gesehen*, the manuscript of which he had entrusted to his sister in January 1945. This extract was entitled "Notes et impressions." In it, he observes a Paris station-restaurant with its typical crowd, and the abandoned Ministry of Foreign Affairs as it was when the Germans moved in, with its hundreds of empty, dusty offices, the chandeliers left burning and the clocks all chiming incessantly in the silence. At night, so as to forget the war and merge with the Paris streets, he puts on civilian clothes. He gives us an account of one of these nocturnal excursions. He takes the métro from Solférino. He gets off at Trinité. The night is dark. It is summer. The air is warm. He walks up the Rue de Clichy in the blackout. On a sofa, in a brothel, he spots a solitary, pathetic Tyrolean hat. The girls file past. "They are in another world, like sleepwalkers, under the effects of chloroform. And everything is bathed"—he writes—"in the eerie light of a tropical aquarium under overheated glass." He too is in another world. He observes everything from a distance, attentive to atmospheres, to tiny, mundane details, and at the same time detached, estranged from everything around him, as though this world at war was no concern of his. Like Friedo Lampe, he died in Berlin in the spring of 1945, at the age of thirty-three, during the final battles, in the carnage and apocalypse of a universe where he had found himself by mistake, wearing a uniform that had been imposed on him but was not his by choice.

And now, why is it that, among so many other writers, my thoughts should turn to the poet Roger Gilbert-Lecomte? He too was struck, in the same period as the two previous writers, as though the few must serve as lightning conductors in order that the others may be spared.

As it happens, our paths had crossed. When I was his age, like him I lived in the southern suburbs of Paris: Boulevard Brune, Rue d'Alésia, Hôtel Primavera, Rue de la Voie-Verte . . . In 1938, he was still there, living near the Porte d'Orléans with a German Jewish girl, Ruth Kronenberg. Then, in 1939, still with her, he moved the short distance to the Plaisance district, to a studio at 16bis Rue Bardinet. The number of times I have taken those streets, without even knowing that Gilbert-Lecomte had been there before me . . . And in 1965, on the Right Bank, in Montmartre, I would spend entire afternoons in a corner café on the Square Caulaincourt and, unaware that Gilbert-Lecomte had also stayed there thirty years earlier, in a hotel off the Rue Caulaincourt: Montmartre 42–99 . . .

About this time, I came across a doctor called Jean Puyaubert. I thought I had a shadow on my lung. To avoid doing military service, I asked him for a certificate. He gave me an appointment at a clinic where he worked in the Place d'Alleray, and had me x-rayed: I had nothing on my lung, I wanted an exemption, and it wasn't as though there was a war on. It was simply that the prospect of barracks life such as I had already been leading in various boarding schools from the ages of eleven to seventeen seemed to me unendurable.

I don't know what became of Dr. Jean Puyaubert. Decades after I had been to see him, I learned that Roger Gilbert-Lecomte had been one of his closest friends, and that the poet, when my age, had asked him the same thing: for a medical certificate confirming that he had had pleurisy—to exempt him from military service.

Roger Gilbert-Lecomte . . . He had dragged out his last years in Paris, under the Occupation . . . In July 1942, his friend, Ruth Kronenberg, was arrested in the Free Zone, on her return from the seaside at Collioure. She was deported in the transport of 11 September, a week before Dora Bruder. A twenty-year-old from Cologne, she had come to Paris some time in 1935 because of racial laws. She enjoyed poetry and the theater. She learned to sew in order to make theatrical costumes. It was no time before she met Roger Gilbert-Lecomte, with other artists in Montparnasse . . .

He continued to live alone in the studio in the Rue Bardinet. Then a Mme Firmat, who had the café opposite, took him in and looked after him. He was a shadow of his former self. In autumn 1942, he undertook several exhausting journeys across the suburbs to Bois-Colombes, where a Dr. Bréavoine in the Rue des Aubépines gave him prescriptions that allowed him to obtain a little heroin. His comings and goings were noted. On 21 October 1942, he was arrested and imprisoned in the Santé. There he remained, in the infirmary, until 19 November. He was released with a summons to appear in court a month later, charged with "having illegally bought prohibited drugs in Paris, Colombes, Bois-Colombes, Asnières, in 1942, and having in his possession heroin, morphine, cocaine . . . "

For a while, in early 1943, he was in a clinic at Épernay, then Mme Firmat put him up in a room above her café. A girl to whom he had lent the studio in the Rue Bardinet during his stay at the clinic, a student, had left behind a box of ampoules containing morphine that he eked out, drop by drop. I never discovered her name.

He died from tetanus on 13 December 1943, at Broussais Hospital, aged thirty-six. Before the war, he had published two collections of poems; one of these books was entitled *La Vie, l'Amour, la Mort, le Vide et le Vent.*

So many friends whom I never knew disappeared in 1945, the year I was born.

As a child, in the apartment at 15 Quai de Conti where my father had lived since 1942—the same apartment that Maurice Sachs[2] had rented the year before—my room overlooked the courtyard. Maurice Sachs relates that he lent these rooms to somebody called Albert, nicknamed "le Zébu."[3] And that he in turn had filled them with "young actors who dreamed of forming a company of their own, and with adolescents who were beginning to write." This "Zébu," Albert Schaky, had the same first name as my father and, like him, came from a family of Italian Jews in Salonika. And like me at the same age exactly thirty years later, he published his first novel with Gallimard, in 1938, at the age of twenty-one, under the name François Vernet. He later joined the Resistance. The Germans arrested him. On the wall of Cell 218, Fresnes, second division, he wrote: "Zébu arrested 10.2.44. Three months on bread

2. Writer and aesthete, Sachs describes his life as a black marketeer during the Occupation in *La Chasse à courre.*

3. A *zébu* is a domestic camel with a muscular hump and sharp horns.

and water, interrogated 9–28 May, visited by doctor 8 June, two days after Allied landing."

He was deported from Compiègne camp on the transport of 2 July 1944 and died in Dachau in March 1945.

Thus, in the apartment where Sachs had carried on his gold trafficking and where, later on, under a false name, my father had hidden, Zébu had occupied my childhood bedroom. Just before I was born, he and others like him had taken all the punishments meted out to them in order that we should suffer no more than pinpricks. I had already worked this out at the age of eighteen while on that journey with my father in the police van, a journey that was a harmless repetition, a parody, of other such journeys—in the same police vans and to the same police stations—but from which nobody had ever returned home, on foot, as I had on that occasion.

I remember, aged twenty-three, late one afternoon on 31 December when, like today, it had grown dark very early, going to see Dr. Ferdière. This man showed me the greatest kindness at a period of my life that, for me, was full of anguish and uncertainty. I vaguely knew that he had admitted Antonin Artaud to the psychiatric hospital at Rodez and had done his best to treat him.[4] But I remember that particular evening for a striking coincidence: I had taken Dr. Ferdière a copy of my first book, *La Place de l'Étoile*, the title of which surprised him.

---

4. Artaud—actor, poet, influential cineaste, and theatrical pioneer—remained in Rodez asylum, in the Free Zone, until 1946; he died in 1948.

He fetched a slim, gray volume from his library to show me: *La Place de l'Étoile* by Robert Desnos,[5] whose friend he was. Dr. Ferdière had had it published himself, in Rodez, a few months after Desnos's death in the camp at Terezin in 1945, the year I was born. I had no idea that Desnos had written a book called *La Place de l'Étoile*. Quite unwittingly, I had stolen his title from him.

---

5. Leading figure in Paris artistic circles, later active in the Resistance.

．．．．．．．．．．．．．．．．．

TWO MONTHS AGO, IN THE ARCHIVES OF THE YIVO IN-
stitute in New York, a friend of mine found the following note among the documentation relating to the former Union Générale des Israélites de France,[1] a body founded under the Occupation:

3L/SBL/

17 JUNE 1942

0032

MEMO TO MLLE SALOMON

Dora Bruder was restored to her mother on the 15th of this month, courtesy of the Clignancourt police.

In view of the fact that she has repeatedly run away, it would seem advisable to remand her to a juvenile home.

The father being interned and the mother in a state of penury, police social workers (Quai de Gesvres) will take the necessary action if required.

Thus, after her return to the maternal domicile on 17 April 1942, Dora Bruder had run away a second time. We have no means of knowing for how long. A month, a month and a half, stolen from the spring of 1942? A week? Where, and in what circumstances, had she been arrested and taken to Clignancourt police station?

---

1. In polite society, *Israélite* was used to avoid the connotations of the word "Jew."

Since 7 June, the wearing of the yellow star had been mandatory. Jews whose names began with A and B had been collecting theirs at police stations since Tuesday 2 June, signing the registers opened for the purpose. Would Dora Bruder have been wearing the star when she was taken to the police station? I doubt it, remembering what her cousin had said about her. A rebel, independent-minded. And besides, in all likelihood she had been on the run long before the beginning of June.

Was she stopped in the street for not wearing the star? I have found the circular dated 6 June 1942 specifying the lot of those picked up for violation of the eighth statute relating to the wearing of the insignia:

From the Directors of the Criminal Investigation Department and the Metropolitan Police:

To Divisional Chief Superintendents, Superintendents of street police for each arrondissement, Superintendents of Paris districts, and all other metropolitan and criminal investigation departments (copies to Directorates of Intelligence Services, Technical Services, Alien and Jewish Affairs . . .

Procedure:

1—*Jews—males aged 18 and over:*

Any Jew in breach of the law shall be remanded to the Dépôt by the street police together with a specific and individual transfer warrant in duplicate (the second copy to be sent to Divisional Superintendent Roux, chief of the Motor Vehicles Department—Dépôt unit). This document is to specify, in addition to the place, day, time, and circumstances of the arrest, the surname, first name, date and place of birth, family status, occupation, domicile, and nationality of the statutory detainee.

2—Jewish females and minors of both sexes aged between 16 and 18 years.

The above shall also be remanded to the Dépôt by the street police under the terms and conditions stated above.

Dépôt personnel are to send the original transfer warrant to the Directorate for Alien and Jewish Affairs, which will rule on each case after consultation with the German authorities. No release may be effected without written orders from the said directorate.

DIRECTORATE OF CRIMINAL INVESTIGATION

TANGUY

DIRECTORATE OF METROPOLITAN POLICE

HENNEQUIN

That June, hundreds of adolescents like Dora were arrested on the street in accordance with Tanguy's and Hennequin's precise and detailed instructions. They passed through the Dépôt and then Drancy on their way to Auschwitz. It goes without saying that the specific and individual transfer warrants of which Superintendent Roux received copies were destroyed after the war, or even, perhaps, as each arrest was completed. All the same, a few remain, inadvertently overlooked.

Police report dated 25 August 1942:

I am dispatching the following to the Dépôt for
failure to wear the Jewish insignia: Sterman Esther, born
13 June 1926, Paris 12th, 42 Rue des Francs-Bourgeois.

Rotsztein Benjamin, born 19 December 1922,
Warsaw, 5 Rue des Francs-Bourgeois, arrested Gare
d'Austerlitz by inspectors of the Intelligence Service,
Section 3.

Police report dated 1 September 1942:

From Inspectors Curinier and Lasalle to the Chief
Superintendent, Special Branch:

We are dispatching Jacobson Louise born Paris
twelfth arrondissement twenty-four December nineteen
hundred twenty-four [. . .] naturalized French nineteen
hundred twenty-five, race Jewish, spinster. Domiciled
with mother, 8 Rue des Boulets, eleventh arrondissement. Student.

Arrested today at approx. fourteen hundred hours
at the maternal domicile in the following circumstances:

The Jacobson girl returned as we were proceeding
with a domiciliary visit at the above address and we
noted that she was not wearing the Jewish insignia in
accordance with a German decree.

She stated that she had left home at eight thirty hours
to study for her *baccalauréat* at the Lycée Henri IV, Rue
Clovis. The girl's neighbors also informed us that she
often went out without wearing the insignia.

Neither we nor the Criminal Investigation Department have any record of the Jacobson girl in our files.

17 May 1944. Yesterday, at 2245 hours, on their rounds, two officers from the 18th arrondissement arrested the French Jew Barmann Jules, born 25 March 1925, Paris, 10th, domiciled 40*bis* Rue du Ruisseau (18th) who being without the yellow star ran away on being questioned by the officers. Having fired three shots without hitting him, the officers effected the arrest on the 8th floor of the apartment building at 12 Rue Charles-Nodier (18th) where he had taken refuge.

But according to the "Memo to Mlle Salomon," Dora Bruder had been returned to her mother. Whether or not she was wearing the star—her mother would have been wearing hers for at least a week—it means that, at Clignancourt police station, she was treated the same as any other runaway girl. Or it may be that the police themselves were responsible for the "Memo to Mlle Salomon."

I have been unable to trace Mlle Salomon. Is she still alive? Evidently, she was a member of UGIF, the organization administered by leading French Israelites who coordinated charity work among the Jewish community during the Occupation. Unfortunately, while the Union Générale des Israélites de France certainly came to the aid of a great many French Jews, its origins were ambiguous: it had been founded on the initiative of the Germans and the Vichy government on the assumption that control of such a body would facilitate their ends, as in the case of the *Judenräte* in the towns and cities of Poland.

Both patrons and staff of the UGIF carried what was called a "legitimization card" to protect them from being rounded up or interned. But this irregular privilege was soon to prove illusory. From 1943 onward, leaders and employees of UGIF were arrested and deported in the hundreds. On the list of these I have found the name of an Alice Salomon, who had worked in the Free Zone. I doubt she could be the Mlle Salomon to whom the memo about Dora was addressed.

Who wrote this memo? If it was somebody on the staff of the UGIF, it suggests that Dora Bruder and her parents had been known to the UGIF for some time. Very likely Cécile Bruder, Dora's mother, in common with the majority of Jews living in extreme poverty with no other means of support, had turned to this organization as a last resort. It was her only means of getting news of her husband, interned at Drancy since March, and of sending him food parcels. And she may have thought that, with the help of the UGIF, she would eventually find her daughter.

"Social workers attached to the police (Quai de Gesvres) will take the necessary action if required." In 1942, these consisted of twenty women attached to the Brigade for the Protection of Minors, a branch of the Criminal Investigation Department. They formed an autonomous section under a senior social worker.

I have found a photograph dating from this period. Two women aged about twenty-five. They are in black—or navy blue—uniform, with a sort of kepi that sports a badge of two intertwined *P*s: Prefecture of Police. The woman on the left, a brunette with hair almost down to her shoulders, carries a satchel. The one on the right appears to be wearing lipstick. Behind the brunette, two wall plaques read: POLICE SOCIAL SERVICES. Below this, an arrow, and underneath it: "Open 0930 h. to 1200 h." The writing on the lower plaque is half obscured by the brunette's head and kepi. Nevertheless, you can read:

DEPARTMENT OF E . . .

INSPECTORS

Underneath, an arrow: "Passage on Right. Door number . . . "
We shall never know the number of this door.

. . . .

WHAT HAPPENED TO DORA, I WONDER, IN THE INTER-
val between 15 June, when she found herself in Clignancourt police station, and 17 June, the date of the "Memo
for Mlle Salomon." Had she been allowed to leave the police
station with her mother?

If she had been allowed to return to the Boulevard Ornano
hotel with her mother—it was no distance, just down the Rue
Hermel—it means that the social workers would have come
for her three days later, after Mlle Salomon had made contact
with the Quai de Gesvres.

But I have a feeling that things were not quite as straight-
forward as that. I have often taken the Rue Hermel, in both
directions, toward the Butte Montmartre and toward the
Boulevard Ornano, and, try as I might, closing my eyes, I find
it hard to picture Dora and her mother walking along this
street on their way back to their hotel room on a sunny June
afternoon as though it was just another day.

I believe that on 15 June, at Clignancourt police station,
Dora and her mother were caught up in a chain reaction over
which they no longer had any control. Children are liable to
expect more from life than their parents and, faced with ad-
versity, their reaction is the more violent. They go farther,
much farther than their parents. And, thereafter, their parents are unable to protect them.

Confronted with the police, Mlle Salomon, social workers,

German decrees and French laws, Cécile Bruder, with her yellow star, her husband interned in Drancy and her "state of penury," would have felt herself utterly defenseless. And quite unable to cope with Dora, who was a rebel and had more than once shown her determination to tear a hole in this net that had been thrown over her and her parents.

"In view of the fact that she has repeatedly run away, it would seem advisable to remand her to a juvenile home."

Perhaps Dora was taken from Clignancourt police station to the Dépôt at police headquarters, that being the usual practice. In which case she would have known that huge, windowless basement, its cells, its straw mattresses heaped with Jewish women, prostitutes, "criminals," and "political" prisoners huddled together anyhow. She would have known the lice, the foul stink, and the wardresses, those terrifying black-clad nuns with little blue veils from whom it was useless to expect the least pity.

Or else she was taken directly to the Quai de Gesvres, open 0930 h. to 1200 h. She went down the passage on the right, stopping outside the door the number of which I shall never know.

Either way, on 19 June 1942, she must have climbed into a police van, where she would have found five girls of her age already installed. Unless these five were picked up as the van did the rounds of police stations. It took them all to the internment center of Tourelles, Boulevard Mortier, at the Porte des Lilas.

THE TOURELLES REGISTER FOR 1942 SURVIVES. ON ITS cover is one word: WOMEN. It listed the names of internees in order of arrival. These women had been arrested for acts of resistance, for being Communists and, up to August 1942, in the case of Jews, for having failed to comply with German decrees: Jews were forbidden to go out after eight o'clock at night, compelled to wear the yellow star, forbidden to cross the demarcation line into the Free Zone, forbidden to use the telephone, to possess a bicycle, a radio . . .

The register has the following entry for 19 June 1942:

> Arrivals 19 June 1942
>
> 439. 19.6.42. Bruder Dora, 25.2.26. Paris 12th.
> French. 41 Bd Ornano. J. xx Drancy 13/8/42.

For the same date, there follow the names of five other girls, all about the same age as Dora:

> 40. 19.6.42. 5th Winerbett Claudine. 26.11.24. Paris
> 9th. French. 82 Rue des Moines. J. xx Drancy 13/8/42.
>
> 1. 19.6.42. 5th Strohlitz Zélie. 4.2.26. Paris 11th.
> French. 48 Rue Molière. Montreuil. J. Drancy 13/8/42.
>
> 2. 19.6.42. Israelowicz Raca. 19.7.1924. Lodz. Ind. J.
> 26 Rue [illegible]. Deported by German authorities
> convoy 19.7.42.
>
> 3. Nachmanowicz Marthe. 23.3.25. Paris. French. 258
> Rue Marcadet. J. xx Drancy. 13/8/42.

4. 19.6.42. 5th. Pitoun Yvonne. 27.1.25. Algiers.
French. 3 Rue Marcel-Sembat. J. xx Drancy 13/8/42.

The police had allotted each girl a registration number. Dora's was 439. I don't know the meaning of 5th. The letter *J* stands for Jewish. Drancy 13/8/42 is added in each case: on 13 August 1942, the day when the three hundred Jewish women who were still interned at Tourelles were transferred to Drancy camp.

ON THAT THURSDAY, 19 JUNE, THE DAY THAT DORA arrived at Tourelles, all the women were assembled on the barracks square after breakfast. Three German officers were present. Jewish women between the ages of eighteen and forty were ordered to line up, backs turned. One of the Germans had ready a complete list of these women and called out their names in the order written. The rest returned to their rooms. The sixty-six women thus segregated from their companions were locked up in a large, empty room without beds or chairs where they remained in isolation for three days, a policeman guarding the door.

On Sunday 22 June, at five o'clock in the morning, buses arrived to take them to Drancy. They were deported the same day, put on a train with over nine hundred men. It was the first transport to leave France with women on board. For the Jewish women in Tourelles, the hovering menace they'd never quite been able to put a name to and, at moments, had succeeded in forgetting, had become fact. And in this oppressive atmosphere Dora spent the first three days of her internment. On the Sunday morning, while it was still dark, she and all her fellow internees watched through closed windows as the sixty-six women were driven away.

On 18 June, or else on the following morning, a desk clerk would have made out Dora's transfer warrant for Tourelles. Had this been done at Clignancourt police station, or at the

Quai de Gesvres? It had had to be made out in duplicate and the copies handed, complete with check marks and signatures, to the guards on the police van. As he signed his name, did the clerk consider the implications of his act? After all, for him, it was merely a routine signature, and besides, the girl was being sent to a place still reassuringly designated by the Prefecture of Police as "Hostel. Supervised short-term accommodation."

I have managed to identify a few of those women who left Tourelles on Sunday 22 June at five o'clock in the morning, and who had come into contact with Dora after her arrival there on the Thursday.

Claude Bloch was thirty-two years old. She had been picked up while on her way to Gestapo headquarters in the Avenue Foch to ask for news of her husband, who had been arrested in December 1941. She was the only person on that transport to survive.

Josette Delimal was twenty-one. Claude Bloch had met her in the Dépôt at police headquarters, and both were taken to Tourelles on the same day. According to Claude, "Josette had had a tough time before the war and hadn't built up the strength you can draw from happy memories. She broke down completely. I did my best to comfort her [. . .]. When they took us to the dormitory to assign us to our beds, I refused to let them separate us. We were together until Auschwitz, where typhus soon carried her off." That's all I know about Josette Delimal. I wish I knew more.

Tamara Isserlis. She was twenty-four. A medical student. She was arrested at Cluny métro station "for concealing the

French flag beneath the star of David." Her identity card has been found and gives her address as 10 Rue de Buzenval, Saint-Cloud. She had an oval-shaped face, light brown hair, and dark eyes.

Ida Levine. Twenty-nine. A few of her letters to her family survive, written first from the Dépôt, then from Tourelles. She threw her last letter from the train at Bar-le-Duc station, where a railroad worker mailed it. She writes: "I'm writing this on a train to an unknown destination, but it's traveling east, so perhaps we're going quite far away . . . "

Hena: I shall call her by her first name. She was nineteen. She had got herself arrested because she and her boyfriend had burgled an apartment, stealing jewelry and cash worth one hundred and fifty thousand old francs. Perhaps, with this money, she dreamed of leaving France and escaping the threats hanging over her. She was taken before a magistrate and sentenced for theft. Being Jewish, she was sent not to an ordinary prison but to Tourelles. I feel a certain solidarity with her act of burglary. In 1942, my father and his accomplices had plundered the SKF warehouse on the Avenue de la Grande-Armée of its stock of ball bearings, loading their loot onto trucks and transporting it back to the den on the Avenue Hoche from which they operated their black market business. According to German decrees, Vichy laws, and articles in the press, they were no better than vermin and common criminals, so they felt justified in behaving like outlaws in order to survive. For them, it was a point of honor. And I applaud them for it.

The rest of what I know about Hena amounts to almost

nothing: she was born on 11 December 1922 at Pruszkow in Poland, and she lived at 42 Rue Oberkampf, the steeply sloping street I have so often climbed.

Annette Zelman. She was twenty-one years old. She was a blonde. She lived at 58 Boulevard de Strasbourg with a young man, Jean Jausion, the son of a professor of medicine. His first poems had been published in *Les Réverbères*, a Surrealist magazine that he had started with some friends just before the war.

Annette Zelman. Jean Jausion. In 1942, they were often to be seen together at the Café de Flore. For a while they had hidden in the Free Zone. Then disaster struck. A few words in a letter from an officer in the Gestapo tell the story:

21 MAY 1942 REFERENCE MARRIAGE BETWEEN JEWS AND NON-JEWS

It has come to my knowledge that the French national Jean Jausion (Aryan), a 24 year-old philosophy student, and the Jewess Anna Melka Zelman, born Nancy on 6 October 1921, plan to marry over the Pentecost holidays.

Jausion's parents wish to prevent this union at all costs but lack the means to do so.

Consequently, I have taken the precaution of ordering the arrest of the Jewess Zelman and her internment in the camp at Tourelles barracks . . .

And a French police file:

Annette Zelman, Jewess, born Nancy 6 October 1921. French: arrested 23 May 1942. Held under lock and key at police headquarters Dépôt from 23 May to 10 June, transferred to Germany 22 June. Reason for arrest: projected marriage to an Aryan, Jean Jausion. Couple signed a written statement renouncing all plans to marry at the express wish of Dr. H. Jausion, who hoped that they would be dissuaded thereby, and that the Zelman girl would be returned to her family without any recriminations.

But this doctor with the strange methods of dissuasion was too trusting: the police failed to return Annette Zelman to her family.

In 1944, Jean Jausion went off to be a war correspondent. In a newspaper dated 11 November 1944, I came across the following announcement:

> Missing. The management of our sister paper *Le Franc-Tireur*[1] would be grateful to anybody having information about the disappearance of one of its contributors, Jean Jausion, born Toulouse 20 August 1917, domiciled Paris, 21 Rue Théodore-de-Banville. Left 6 September on an assignment for *Franc-Tireur*, accompanied by a young couple named Lecomte, former maquisards, in a black Citroën 11, front-wheel drive, license number RN 6283, bearing a white *Franc-Tireur* sticker at the rear.

---

1. An underground Resistance newspaper published openly after the liberation of Paris in August 1944.

I heard that Jean Jausion launched his car at a German infantry column. He fired a machine gun at them until they had a chance to shoot back and give him the death that he had sought.

A book by Jean Jausion came out the following year, in 1945. It was entitled *Un Homme marche dans la ville.*

TWO YEARS AGO, ON ONE OF THE BOOKSTALLS ALONG the Seine, I happened to find the last letter written by a man who was on the transport of 22 June with Claude Bloch, Josette Delimal, Tamara Isserlis, Hena, Jean Jausion's girl-friend, Annette . . .

The fact that the letter was for sale, like any other manu-script, suggests that the sender and his family had disappeared in their turn. A square of thin paper covered back and front in minuscule handwriting. It was written from Drancy camp by a certain Robert Tartakovsky. I've discovered that he was born in Odessa on 24 November 1902, and that, before the war, he wrote a column on art for *Illustration*. Today, fifty years later, on Wednesday, 29 January 1997, I reproduce his letter.

19 JUNE 1942. FRIDAY.

MADAME TARTAKOVSKY

50 RUE GODEFROY-CAVAIGNAC. PARIS XIe

Yesterday I was picked to go. I've been mentally prepared for a long time. The camp is panic-stricken, many men are crying, they are afraid. The only thing bothering me is that most of the clothes I keep asking for still haven't arrived. I sent off a coupon for a clothes parcel: will what I need come in time? I don't want my mother or any of you to

worry. I'll do my utmost to keep safe and well. If you don't
hear from me, be patient, if necessary, go to the Red Cross.
Ask the Saint-Lambert police (town hall XVe), Vaugiraud
métro, to return the documents seized on 3/5. Be sure
and ask about my certificate of voluntary enlistment,
Regimental no. 10107, it may be at the camp and I don't
know if they'll let me have it back. Please take a cast of
Albertine to Mme BIANOVICI, *14 Rue Deguerry, Paris XIe,*
it's for a friend in my hut. She'll give you 1,200 francs for
it. Write first to be sure of finding her in. I approached M.
Gompel,[1] an internee at Drancy, and the sculptor is to be
invited to exhibit at Les Trois Quartiers. Should the gallery
want the entire edition, keep back three casts, saying either
that they've been sold or else reserved for the publisher. You
can make two extra casts following said request if you think
the mold will bear it. Don't distress yourselves too much. I
wish Marthe to go on vacation. Never think that no news
means bad news. If you get this note in time, send the
maximum number of food parcels, moreover the weight
will be less carefully checked. Anything glass will be sent
back, and we are forbidden knives, forks, razor-blades,
pens, etc. Even needles. But I'll manage somehow. Army
biscuits or unleavened bread welcome. In one of my regular
notecards I mentioned a friend PERSIMAGI, *see Swedish*
Embassy on his behalf (Irène), he's even taller than me and

---

1. Roger Gompel was the director of a chain of department stores, including Les
Trois Quartiers. He was interned at Drancy but later released.

*his clothes are in tatters (see Gattégno, 13 Rue Grande-
Chaumière). A bar or two of good soap, some shaving soap,
a shaving brush, toothbrush, nailbrush, all welcome, I'm
trying to think of everything at once, to mix the practical
with all the other things I have to say to you. Nearly a
thousand of us are to go. There are also Aryans in the
camp. They are forced to wear the Jewish insignia. SS
Captain Doncker arrived at the camp yesterday, scattering
people in all directions. Advise our friends to get away
somewhere if they can, for here one must abandon all hope.
We may be sent to Compiègne before we leave for good, I'm
not sure. I won't be sending back any laundry, I'll do it
here. The cowardice of most people here appals me. What
will be its effect once we're there, I wonder. If you can, go
and see Mme de Salzman, not to ask her for anything in
particular, just for information. Perhaps I'll get a chance to
meet the person whom Jacqueline wanted to get released.
Urge my mother to be very careful, people are being
arrested daily, some here are very young, 17, 18, others as
old as 72. Up to Monday morning, you can send parcels
here as often as you like. It's not true that they no longer
accept parcels at the usual addresses, don't take no for an
answer, telephone the UGIF at the Rue de la Bienfaisance. I
didn't mean to alarm you in my previous letters, was only
surprised not to have received the clothes I'll need for the
journey. I'll be sending my watch back for Marthe,
probably also my pen, I'll entrust these to B. Put nothing
perishable in food parcels in case things have to be for-*

warded to me. *Photographs without letters in food parcels or underwear. I'll probably send back the art books for which my warmest thanks. Doubtless I'll be spending the winter there, don't worry, I'm prepared. Reread my cards. You'll see which things I've been asking for from the first and have slipped my mind. Darning wool. Scarf. Sterogyl 15. My mother's metal box, as sugar crumbles. What upsets me is that all deportees have their heads shaved, it makes you even more conspicuous than the insignia. In the event of dispersal, I'll go on sending news via the Salvation Army, let Irène know.*

SATURDAY 20 JUNE 1942.—*My dear ones, case arrived yesterday, thank you for everything. I'm not sure, but I fear a hurried departure. I am to have my head shaved today. From tonight, deportees will probably be confined to a special hut and closely guarded, even to the lavatory and back. A sinister atmosphere hovers over the camp. I doubt that we'll be going via Compiègne. I know we are to be given three days' rations for the journey. I'm afraid I'll be gone before more parcels arrive, but don't worry, the last one was very generous and since being here I've put aside all chocolate and jams, and the large sausage. Keep calm, I'll be thinking of you. I wanted to give Marthe the records of* Petrouchka *on 28/7, the complete set is 4 r. Saw B. last night to thank him for all he has done, he knows I've been defending Leroy's sculptures to key people here. Am delighted with latest photos of the works but haven't shown them to B., apologized for not giving him one but said he could always ask you. Sad to interrupt the edition, but there's still time if I get back soon. I like Leroy's work, would gladly have brought out a reduction within my means, can't stop thinking about it, even though we are to leave in a few hours.*

Please do all you can for my mother, by which I don't mean that you should neglect your personal affairs. Tell Irène that as she is her neighbour I wish her to do likewise. Try to telephone Dr. André ABADI *(if still in Paris). Tell him that I met the person whose address he knows on 1 May and was arrested on 3 May (was it simple coincidence?). The incoherence of this note probably surprises you; but the atmosphere is hard to bear, it's 6:30* A.M. *I'm about to send back everything I'm not taking with me, I'm afraid of taking too much. The searchers are liable to throw out a case at the last moment if there's no room, it depends on their mood (they belong to the Jewish Affairs police, either fascists or anti-Semites). Still, that has its uses. I'll get my belongings sorted out. Don't panic the moment you stop hearing from me, keep calm, wait patiently and with trust, have faith in me, reassure my mother that, having seen departures for the Beyond (as I told you), I prefer to be on this journey. My main regret is to be parted from my pen, not to be allowed paper (an absurd thought crosses my mind: knives are forbidden, and I don't even possess a simple key to a can of sardines). I'm not putting on a brave face, don't have the heart in this atmosphere: a lot of the sick and infirm are also picked for deportation. I'm also thinking of Rd, hoping that he is safe at last. I had all sorts of things with Jacques Daumal. Probably no point in moving my books out of the house now, I leave it to you. Let's hope we have good weather for the journey! Make sure my mother receives all her allowances, get the UGIF to help her. I hope you've made it up with Jacqueline by now, she is a strange girl, but good at heart (the sky is clearing, it's going to be a fine day). I don't know if you got my usual card, or if I'll get an answer before we leave. I think of my mother, of you. Of all my loving friends who did so much to help me keep my freedom. Heartfelt thanks to those who helped me "get through" the winter. I'm leaving this letter unfinished. It's time to pack my bag. Back soon. A note in case I can't finish, pen and watch are for Marthe whatever my mother says. I kiss you good-bye dearest Maman, and you my dear ones, with all my love. Be brave. It's 7 A.M., back soon.*

. . . .

TWICE IN APRIL 1966 I SPENT A SUNDAY IN THE EASTERN
districts of Paris, looking for some trace of Dora Bruder
in the areas around the Saint-Coeur-de-Marie and Tourelles.
I felt this was best done on a Sunday, when the town is deserted, at the lowest ebb of the tide.

Nothing is left of the Saint-Coeur-de-Marie. A modern
apartment block stands at the corner of the Rue de Picpus and
the Rue de la Gare-de-Reuilly. The section that has replaced
the school's tree-shaded wall now displays the last odd numbers in the Rue de la Gare-de-Reuilly. Opposite, a little further along on the even-numbered side, the street is unchanged.

It's hard to believe that one July morning in 1942, while
Dora was interned at Tourelles, the police had come to arrest
nine young children and adolescents at number 48*bis,* where
the windows overlooked the garden of the Saint-Coeur-de-
Marie. It's a five-story building in light-colored brick. On each
floor, two windows flank two smaller windows. Number 40
next door is a grayish building, recessed. In front of it, a low
brick wall with an iron gate. Other small houses opposite, on
the same side as the perimeter wall of the old boarding school,
have remained as they were. Number 54, just before you reach
the Rue de Picpus, used to be a café owned by a Mlle Lenzi.

All of a sudden, I felt certain that, on the night when she
had made her escape, Dora had slipped away from the board-

ing school by the Rue de la Gare-de-Reuilly. I visualized her, hugging the school wall. Perhaps streets named after a station evoke thoughts of escape.

I wandered around for a while, and then the sadness of those other Sundays when it was time to return to the boarding school began to weigh me down. I felt sure that she left the métro at Nation. She put off the moment when she must enter the gate and cross the courtyard. She prolonged her walk, choosing streets at random. It grew dark. The Avenue de Saint-Mandé is quiet, bordered by trees. I forget if there is open ground. You pass the entrance to the old Picpus métro station. Did she ever emerge from there? In comparison with the Avenue de Saint-Mandé, the Avenue de Picpus, on the right, is cold and desolate. Treeless, I seem to remember. But the solitude of returning, on those Sunday evenings.

The Boulevard Mortier is a hill. It slopes southward. On my way there, that Sunday of 28 April 1996, I took the following route: Rue des Archives, Rue de Bretagne, Rue des Filles-du-Calvaire. Then the hill of the Rue Oberkampf, where Hena had lived.

To the right, the Rue des Pyrénées, offering a vista of trees. Rue de Ménilmontant. The apartment blocks at number 140 lay deserted in the glare of the sun. For the last part of the Rue Saint-Fargeau, I seemed to be traversing an abandoned village.

Plane trees line the Boulevard Mortier. At the top, just before you reach the Porte des Lilas, the old Tourelles barracks are still there.

On that particular Sunday, the boulevard was empty, lost in a silence so deep that I could hear the rustling of the plane trees. The buildings of the former barracks are hidden behind a high perimeter wall. I followed it. Affixed to it was a sign that read:

MILITARY ZONE

FILMING OR PHOTOGRAPHY PROHIBITED

I told myself that nobody remembers anything anymore. Behind the wall there lay a no-man's-land, a zone of emptiness and oblivion. Unlike the boarding school in the Rue de Picpus, the twin blocks of Tourelles barracks had not been pulled down, but they might as well have been.

And yet, from time to time, beneath this thick layer of amnesia, you can certainly sense something, an echo, distant, muted, but of what, precisely, it is impossible to say. Like finding yourself on the edge of a magnetic field, with no pendulum to pick up the radiation. Out of suspicion and a guilty conscience they had put up the sign, "Military zone. Filming or photography forbidden."

....

IN A DIFFERENT PART OF PARIS, WHEN I WAS TWENTY, I
remember having the same sensation of emptiness as I had
had when confronted by the Tourelles wall, without knowing
the reason why.

I had a girlfriend who lived in various borrowed flats and
country houses. I regularly took advantage of this to relieve
their libraries of art books and numbered editions, which I
then sold. One day, when we were by ourselves in a flat on the
Rue du Regard, I stole an antique music box and also, after
rifling the closets, several very smart suits, a few shirts, and
about ten pairs of handmade shoes. I searched the yellow
pages for a secondhand dealer to whom I could resell these
items and found one in the Rue des Jardins-Saint-Paul.

This street leads up from the Quai des Célestins on the
Seine and intersects the Rue de Charlemagne near the school
where, the year before, I had gone through the ordeal of my
baccalauréat. One of the last buildings on the right just before
the Rue de Charlemagne had a rusting iron curtain at street
level, half raised. I pushed my way into a junkshop piled high
with furniture, clothes, ironwork, automobile parts. The
forty-year-old man who greeted me was most obliging, offering to come and collect the "goods" in a few days' time.

Having taken my leave of him, I walked down the Rue des
Jardins-Saint-Paul toward the Seine. All the buildings on the
lefthand side of the street had been pulled down not long be-

fore. As had the other buildings behind them. In their place, nothing but a wasteland, itself surrounded by half-demolished walls. On these walls, open to the sky, you could still make out the patterned paper of what was once a bedroom, the trace of a chimney. You would have said that the district had been hit by a bomb, and the vista of the Seine at the bottom of the street only increased the impression of emptiness.

On the following Sunday, by appointment, the secondhand dealer came to my girlfriend's father's place on the Boulevard Kellermann, near the Porte de Gentilly, where I was to hand over the "goods." He loaded music box, suits, shirts, and shoes on to his van, giving me seven hundred old francs for the lot.

He suggested going for a drink. We stopped at one of two cafés opposite Charlety stadium.

He asked me what I did for a living. I didn't quite know what to say. In the end, I told him that I had dropped out of school. I questioned him in return. The junkshop in the Rue de Jardins-Saint-Paul belonged to his cousin, who was also his business partner. He himself had another, near the flea market at the Porte de Clignancourt. It turned out that he came from a local family of Polish Jews.

I was the one who brought up the subject of the war and the Occupation. He was eighteen at the time. He remembered that, one Saturday, the police had made a swoop on the Saint-Ouen flea market to round up the Jews, and he had escaped by a miracle. What had shocked him most was that one of the police inspectors had been a woman.

I told him about the wasteland stretching to the foot of the apartment blocks on the Boulevard Ney that I had noticed on the Saturdays when my mother took me to the flea markets. That was the place where he and his family had lived. Rue Élisabeth-Rolland. He was surprised that I should make a note of its name. A district known as the Plain. Completely demolished after the war, it was now a playing field.

Talking to him, I thought of my father, whom I hadn't seen for a long time. When he was nineteen, my age, before he lost himself in dreams of high finance, my father had lived by wheeling and dealing at the gates of Paris: he smuggled drums of gasoline for resale to garage owners, liquor, and various other goods. All without paying excise tax.

As we parted, he said in a friendly way that if I had any more items for him, I could contact him at the Rue des Jardins-Saint-Paul. And he gave me an extra hundred francs, no doubt touched by my air of being a guileless, likeable young chap.

I've forgotten his face. I remember nothing about him, apart from his name. He could easily have met Dora Bruder, around the Porte de Clignancourt, around the Plain. They were the same age and lived in the same neighborhood. Perhaps he knew the full story of the times she spent on the run . . . The fact is, there are flukes, encounters, coincidences, and we shall never take advantage of them . . . I was thinking of that, this autumn, when I went back to explore the area around the Rue des Jardins-Saint-Paul. The junkshop with its iron curtain was no more, and the buildings nearby had been restored. Once again, I had a sense of emptiness. And I understood why. After the war, most buildings in the area had been pulled down, methodically, in accordance with a government plan. Due for demolition, this zone had even been allotted a name and number: Block 16. I have found some photographs. One shows the Rue des Jardins-Saint-Paul with the houses on the lefthand side still standing. Another, the half-demolished buildings beside Saint-Gervais church and around the Hôtel de Sens. Another, a wasteland along the banks of the Seine, with people crossing it between two now useless sidewalks: all that remains of the Rue des Nonnains-d'Hyères. And here, on this wasteland, they have put up row upon row of houses, altering the course of an old street in the process.

The facades are rectangular, the windows square, the concrete the color of amnesia. The street lamps throw out a cold light. Here and there, a decorative touch, some artificial flowers: a bench, a square, some trees. They have not been content with putting up a sign like that on the wall of Tourelles barracks: "No filming or photography." They have obliterated everything in order to build a sort of Swiss village in order that nobody, ever again, would question its neutrality.

The patches of wallpaper that I had seen thirty years ago in the Rue des Jardins-Saint-Paul were remnants of former rooms—rooms that had been home to young people of Dora's age until the day when the police had come for them in July 1942. The list of their names is always associated with the same streets. And the street names and house numbers no longer correspond to anything at all.

．．．．．．．．．．．．．．．．

WHEN I WAS SEVENTEEN, TOURELLES HAD MEANT NO more than a name I had read at the back of a book by Jean Genet, *Miracle de la Rose*. There, he lists the places where the book was written: LA SANTÉ, TOURELLES PRISON 1943. Shortly after Dora Bruder's departure from Tourelles, he too had been imprisoned there, as a common criminal, and their paths may have crossed. *Miracle de la Rose* is not only impregnated with memories of the penal settlement at Mettray— one of those juvenile homes where they had wanted to send Dora—but also, I now realize, of La Santé and Tourelles.

I know sentences from this book by heart. I remember one in particular: "What that child taught me is that the true roots of Parisian slang lie in its sad tenderness." This phrase evokes Dora Bruder for me so well that I feel I knew her. The children with Polish or Russian or Rumanian names who were forced to wear the yellow star, were so Parisian that they merged effortlessly into the facades, the apartment blocks, the sidewalks, the infinite shades of gray that belong to Paris alone. Like Dora Bruder, they all spoke with the Parisian accent, using a slang whose sad tenderness Jean Genet had recognized.

At Tourelles, when Dora was a prisoner there, you could receive parcels, and also visits, on Thursdays and Sundays. And, on Tuesdays, you could attend Mass. The guards held roll call at eight o'clock in the morning. The detainees stood to attention at the end of their beds. For lunch, in the refectory, there was nothing but cabbage. Exercise period on the barracks square. Supper at six o'clock. Another roll call. Every two weeks, a trip to the shower, two at a time, accompanied by a guard. Whistle blasts. You waited. To receive a visit, you had to write a letter to the prison director, and you never knew if he would give his authorization.

Visits took place after lunch, in the refectory. Those who came had their bags searched by the guards. Parcels were opened. Often, for no reason, visits were canceled, and detainees informed only an hour beforehand.

Among the women whom Dora could have met at Tourelles were some who were known to the Germans as "Jews' friends": there were about ten of them, "Aryan" Frenchwomen, who, from the first day in June when Jews were obliged to wear the yellow star, had had the courage to wear it themselves out of solidarity but did so in imaginative ways that ridiculed the occupying authorities. One had fixed the yellow star to the collar of her dog. Another embroidered hers with PAPOU.[1] Another, with JENNY. Another attached stars to her belt, each bearing a letter, spelling out the word VICTOIRE. All were picked up in the street and taken to the nearest police station. Then to the Dépôt at police headquarters. Then to Tourelles.

---

1. A native of Papua, New Guinea.

Then, on 13 August, to Drancy camp. Between them, these "friends of Jews" had the following occupations: Typist. Stationer. Newsdealer. Cleaner. Postal worker. Student.

In August the number of arrests multiplied. Women no longer even passed through the Dépôt but were taken directly to Tourelles. Dormitories meant for twenty now held double that number. With the overcrowding, it was suffocatingly hot, and anxiety mounted. It was common knowledge that Tourelles was merely a holding yard where, from one day to the next, you might be shunted off to an unknown destination.

Two groups of Jewish women, about a hundred in all, had already left for Drancy camp on 19 and 27 July. Among them, an eighteen-year-old Pole, Raca Israelowicz, who had arrived at Tourelles on the same day as Dora, probably in the same police van. And who was doubtless one of her neighbors in the dormitory.

On the evening of 12 August, a rumor spread through Tourelles that all Jewish women and "Jews' friends"were to leave for Drancy camp on the following day.

At ten o'clock on the morning of 13 August, the interminable roll call began under the chestnut trees on the barracks square. A last meal. A meager ration that left you famished.

The buses arrived. In sufficient number—apparently—for each prisoner to have a seat. Dora included. It was a Thursday, visiting day.

The convoy set out. It was escorted by helmeted policemen

on motorcycles. It took the route that you follow today for the Roissy airport. More than fifty years have passed. By building a highway, razing houses to the ground, and transforming the landscape of this northeastern suburb, they have rendered it, like the former Block 16, as neutral and gray as possible. But the blue road signs on the road to the airport still bear the old names: DRANCY or ROMAINVILLE. And, stranded and forgotten on the shoulder of the highway, near the Porte de Bagnolet, there is an old wooden barn on which someone has painted this name, clearly visible: DUREMORD.

At Drancy, among the milling crowds, Dora found her father. He had been interned there since March. That particular August, as in the Dépôt at police headquarters, as at Tourelles, the camp filled up day by day with an increasing flood of men and women. Some came in the thousands by freight train from the Free Zone. Many hundreds of women, forcibly separated from their children, came from the camps at Pithiviers and Beaune-la-Rolande. And, from 15 August onward, after their mothers had been deported, the children arrived in turn, four thousand of them. In many cases their names, hastily scribbled on their clothes before they left Pithiviers and Beaune-la-Rolande, were no longer legible. Unidentified child no. 122. Unidentified child no. 146. Girl aged three. First name Monique. Unidentified.

Because of the overcrowding in the camp, and in anticipation of the convoys still to arrive from the Free Zone, on 2 and 5 September the authorities decided to transfer Jews of

French nationality from Drancy to Pithiviers. Four girls who had arrived at Tourelles on the same day as Dora—Claudine Winerbett, Zélie Strohlitz, Marthe Nachmanowicz, and Yvonne Pitoun—all aged sixteen or seventeen, left on this convoy of some fifteen hundred French Jews. They were probably under the illusion that their nationality would protect them. Dora, being French, could have left with them. The reason she didn't do so is easy to guess: she preferred to stay with her father.

Father and daughter departed Drancy on 18 September, in company with thousands of other men and women, on a convoy of trains bound for Auschwitz.

Dora's mother, Cécile Bruder, was arrested on 16 July 1942, the day of the great roundup, and interned at Drancy. She was reunited with her husband for a few days while their daughter was at Tourelles. Doubtless because she was born in Budapest and the authorities had not yet received orders to deport Hungarian Jews, Cécile Bruder was released from Drancy on 25 July.

Had she been able to visit Dora at Tourelles, one Thursday or Sunday, during that summer of 1942? On 9 January 1943, she was once again interned in Drancy camp and, on 11 February 1943, five months after her husband and daughter, she was put on a convoy for Auschwitz.

On Saturday 19 September, the day after Dora and her father left, the occupying authorities imposed a curfew in retaliation